Nine Realms

Book One

In The Series

~For Goblins' Sake~

To Emma...

AB

Nine Realms

~For Goblins' Sake~
Book One

A.K. Baxter

Mount Willow Books

The Nine Realm series are stand-alone books, and are a work of fiction. Names, places, characters and events are all created by the author's imagination and do not resemble real people living or dead. Locations and public sites used are created for the story alone and any resemblance of places, people, or things are coincidental.

Middle Grade Fantasy Novella
Nine Realms: Book One- For Goblins' Sake
Issued in print and electronic formats
ISBN: 978-1-7752053-0-2 (paperback)
ISBN: 978-1-7752053-1-9 (kindle)

Printed in USA

First Edition: January 2018

DEDICATION

I dedicate this book to my son, Patrick, whose imagination and positivity has encouraged me to write this story. Also, to my second son, due in the new year of 2018, who has given me a nudge in the right direction, to get this book completed.

    To my husband, Jason, for his constant support and ability to motivate me. Over the past two years, he has become my chauffer, driving me through the Rocky Mountains for inspiration and some mental clarity. He has been involved in as much of the process as I have, so I am eternally grateful for his patience ... and this is just the beginning of the series.

ACKNOWLEDGMENTS

To Ariane R. Kamps for your beautiful illustration of the Nine Realms.

To Taylor Cummings, for your artwork and skill throughout this journey.

To Ron. B. Saunders, fellow author and creator of The Aurykon Chronicles, for your editing help, generosity, and kind words.

To Brian Tedesco, for your editing and support.

A.K. BAXTER

CONTENTS

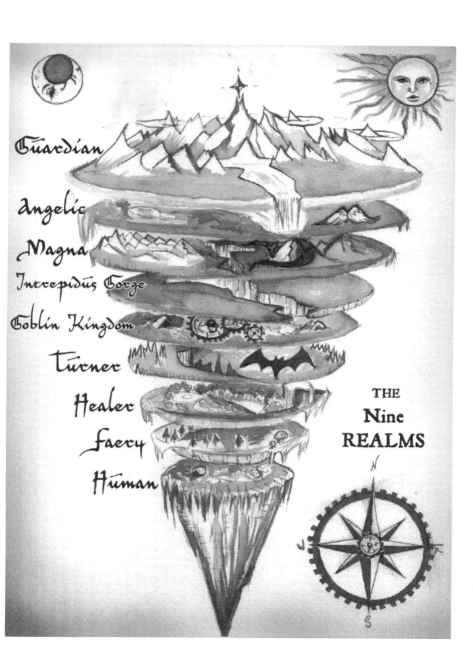

Guardian

Angelic

Magna

Intrepidus Gorge

Goblin Kingdom

Turner

Healer

Faery

Human

THE
Nine
REALMS

The Nine Realms

- ❖ In the centre of the nine is, of course, the Goblin Kingdom, with the most important job of all, maintaining the magic.
- ❖ The highest realm named the Guardian Realm, home to the spirits, ancestors, shamans, spirit animals, and occasionally the tooth faeries.
- ❖ The Angelic Realm, home to the elves and the elders.
- ❖ Then there is the Magna Realm, or you may know it as the mythology realm, of all things wonderful, including dragons, and gods of old and new.

- Intrepidus Gorge, beholds the giants, ogres, and trolls. Creatures feared, yet with a soul as pure as the elves.
- Turners have their own realm within the underworld: the werewolves, the vampires, shapeshifters and naguals.
- Kingdom of Healers. We are all connected to this kingdom, even you but only those creatures that pursue a life of healing reside here, like the dwarfs, animals, and trees.
- The Faery Realm and protectors of nature live among those tricky pixies and the brownies.
- The Human Realm, home to the Goboids and Earthlings. Also known as the grounders. All creatures wander through this realm and their own, discreetly.

0: THE MAGICAL ENGINEERS

In the realms of all existence lie many layers of creatures, magic, and curiosity. To the human eye, with limited sight, only the land you know exists, right? Of course, your imagination can see far more than your eye, but few of you allow yourselves to submerge deep enough to believe it. You may have read about mythical creatures, faeries, and goblins, but they are only stories to you, but to me, it's my life. I am a Phoenix.

Have you ever heard your pets meow and bark

with an intense scowl when there is nothing there? What scuttles in dark shadows or gives you pins and needles? Well, I expect it's the creatures of the nine, or more specifically, goblins.

Yes, they may be ugly, they may be dirty, they may lurk in dark corners, but they are the ones— the only ones—that can keep the rest of us alive. It is their job and lifelong undertaking to maintain, feed, and protect the magic within the core of the realms. They are born from pure magic and are hardworking creatures—who have miraculously created an underground maze deep into the Earth's crust, where their headquarters are forged in the hot core of Mother Earth.

You see, I am a watcher, or messenger, if you like, who takes pride in understanding people and learning the human ways. You are rather remarkable beings, full of emotions.

You could say that every time a child prays and wishes to see faeries, creatures, or mythical beings, I hear them first and then send that message on to the source personally. So please, children, don't judge the messenger, I am simply the creator's secretary.

With the human population increasing and interfering with the unknown, the realm's magic weakens, so they rely even more on the goblins' protection and magic source. The cog's power must be protected.

It seems that a little box known as a "TV" controls your daily actions and thoughts. Ever since the incident with the flying dragon spotted in Bulgaria, the news has bent the truth and exploited our own.

You have likely learned that crime rates are at a high and blamed on us, the creatures of the nine, but I can tell you that it is not our doing. It is you humans that are in control of your own actions.

We creatures like to take a back seat and maintain that magic within us all.

The goblins are there for your protection as well as ours, but their life is full of the cog's power and darkness, hunting, and engineering. As you could imagine, they may get bored or want to wander off to the realms of the unicorns or the woodland free-flyers. This is exactly what happened to one goblin,

Alchom Darkblood, head engineer/science technician. Through boredom, he carried out scientific experiments of the kind that are banned—the type that could cause great danger to the entire world, even for you. He mixed human DNA with goblin DNA. With the access to the greatest magic on Earth and all the realms, he created a tiny newborn goboid with the strength of man and magic of a goblin.

This brought great chaos to the world, even killing off a breed of goblins—the Peedie Folk—the ones that discreetly help in your homes. I am sure you've heard of these myths before, unfortunately, that is what they have now become due to the sloppy, boorish ways of the goblins. The only difference between the Peedie Folk goblins and the engineering goblins is that the latter have allergies.

Unfortunately, they don't get out much, which had led to a low immune system, and allergies are rather common in the underground cog's maze, since the demise of the Peedie Folk. After the humans feared the goblins ulterior motive was to steal their children and create half-breeds, you could imagine the humans began to fight back, which led to the Peedie Folk's unfortunate end.

Today, the fear is rising, and goboids are coming of age and experimenting with their goblin powers. Havoc, fear, and chaos are what cause your crime rates to increase, your bizarre nightmares, your memory loss, and your missing pets and even the loss of loved ones.

I am telling you this because you will most likely forget what I have told you in the morning anyway. If you are in possession of any half-breeds, be warned, they are hardwired to erase any memory that may put their true identity at risk.

1: THE DROP-OFF

The trees writhed as if a dragon had stormed through the town on this blusterous evening, leaving debris and an eerie echo in that hollow street.

A darkness had harnessed and interrupted the geyser's stream of magic, deep in the goblins' cog maze.

I could sense a change was about to happen, the sorts of which I was not too keen on overlooking, but be it my job to be the messenger, I was forced to watch it all.

An unsettling vibration wafted through the

realms of the mythical ones. The creatures of all sizes twitched and anxiously awaited for a settling moment, but that moment did not come. Magic was on the brink of becoming purely engineered rather than pure.

****

On a similar morning, a howl blew through that town—cats bellowed and dogs yelped at the shadows that haunted around.

There was a scuttling at a doorway— a rather welcoming one, with red brick forming an archway and candlestick holders on either side. No lights were on. This house belonged to the Fox family, very well off, with well-behaved children.

The family have no desire in meddling with the under realms, nor interfering with the likes of faery magic, or dragon hunting, or even goblin spotting. These children are Nora and Jeremiah, or Jerry for short—which is what he calls himself.

The scuttle at the doorway was not nearly loud enough to wake anybody from their human slumber, but the cats' *shriek* on the other claw was what did the trick.

The mother one, named Wanda, fair as they come, beautiful she was and a writer, but not the sort that writes about my kind, thankfully. Dressed in a white gown, she floated down the staircase like an angel, I mean ... a woman. If the angels heard me say that, I may be demoted.

She eased the door open, half-asleep and unaware of the time. She checked outside, but there was no sign of anyone, only the streetlights flickering. A loud cry shrilled, and she shooed the cat away out of fright, but it was not the cat.

Just before she was about to close the door, it cried again ... Wanda turned around and gasped.

"A baby!"

Someone had left a baby on their doorstep. Wrapped in a dirty cloth, the basket was meticulously weaved from grass, and clay held it together.

Wanda picked up the basket and took it into her home without a second thought.

There had been a lot of snooping and research taken upon this family by my kind. It seemed to be that they were a kind and loving family, the typical type you see on your TV boximecallsits.

It was as if nothing could go wrong with them—city life, school, and family holidays, pets galore, and simple adventures. The father was a mechanic, inclined to fix everything and make it all better, even children. Every morning at 8 am, he would sit in his spot at the bottom of the garden, on a bench he built himself, and read the newspaper. Whether it was rain or shine, he would take at least ten minutes and sit, pondering by himself.

Nora was six, the eldest, and Jerry, also six, twins. Born 6.32 minutes apart, and have argued ever since.

That night the baby's cry woke the whole family up. The animals scuttled away, and the children were not amused.

"What is that?" asked Greg.

Wanda grinned, with tears of happiness in her eyes. She was speechless but mustered a squeal.

"It's a baby!"

"I can see that, but where did it come from? Why is it here?" asked Greg.

Jerry interrupted. "It's a girl, not an 'it', Dad."

"We can't keep it," said Nora, wiping the sleep from her eyes.

"We must, we are all she's got," said Wanda. "Look at her dinky turned-up nose, she's beautiful."

Mother and father glanced at each other with a wistful sigh. No one got much sleep that night.

Nora and Jerry were both the quiet type, kept to themselves, and cared rarely for toys, or each other for that matter.

"I don't like this. Why couldn't they ask us if we want another sister?" Nora huffed and retreated to her book.

"It's not always about you!" he said, "I think it will be good for us, give us something to look forward to."

"We don't need any more excitement with you in and out of hospital," Nora snarled. She seldom received any sort of attention any more.

"It's just asthma, not life threatening, and she's just a baby." Jerry yawned. "It's too late for this rubbish."

"Well," said Nora, "Perhaps having another

sister will get you out of the bushes more."

"Nothing wrong with liking the outdoors. Better than sulking and reading books all the time."

Nora switched her bedside lamp off and said, "School tomorrow. Night!"

It wasn't until I overheard the goblins' conversation, that I realised their plan may have gone more smoothly than they thought.

Usually, when a child is deposited on a doorstep the stalk is blamed or another human being, never the goblins, because surely, how would they manage to get their grubby hands on one?

The usual questions and worry about what they would do with a baby came up in conversation—do we report it to the police? Should we leave her on someone else's doorstep? Yes, that's been done before! Or should we just accept her as our own? That is exactly what they did.

"Its fate," said Wanda, "you know, with you not being able to have children anymore, I think we're supposed to have this child."

"It is rather convenient, said Greg, "only a month after the doctor tells me I can't have children and you desperately want one. Have you been meddling again?"

"Oh, why do you always assume something bad is going to happen? Can't you just accept it as fate?"

Greg grunted, knowing she was right. It was something we noticed buried deep within him, an uncontrollable negative mindset. He must be a troll descendant.

We knew this family would be an easy target—drop a baby bomb on their doorstep, and it was almost definitely, at least fifty percent guaranteed that they would take her in, no questions asked.

Since the goblins were desperate to get rid of the baby for good, the most suitable home had to be found. The baby's gender seemed to cause the problem. The goblins always need an extra pair of hands to help underground, but a *female*—goblins despised them. They are their own breed according to the goblins. Very old fashioned if you ask me—haven't quite got out of the dark ages but are capable of constructing a sophisticated underworld maze that is engineered to harness the magic and time of the universe—genius. I suppose there has to be some give when it comes to their ways.

Unfortunately, any females that are born from the banned, yet regular scientific experiments are disposed and abandoned in the human realm until they come of age.

The scientist goblin that performs these little naughty experiments is sly. He hunts for the human DNA by night, creeping into your rooms and sniffing out your blood. Unfortunately, their sense of smell is not that great, unlike mine. I can detect a female from miles away, but the goblins are somewhat simple and can't differentiate between male and female humans, so they end up creating a variety of mixed breeds. Sometimes they are born looking more goblin, and others more human, which is the case for baby Clara, which is what they named her, after Wanda's mother.

Clara was exactly two days old when abandoned on the doorstep, not a single visible goblin feature about her. Her nose slightly turned up, all the better for sniffing out cats. She had greeny-blue eyes, which changed in the light. No one ever mentioned the fact that she was left on a doorstep. A rule set that Clara must never know, and she was to grow up believing she was their biological daughter. After the demise of the Peedie Folk, humans had no need to suspect half-breeds existed anymore.

So, the rumours in the news were presumed lies or myths recreated. There was no proof behind the stories.

With goblin's work becoming harder and more dangerous, magic had to be engineered deep within the depths of the harsh core. The punishment that the scientists bestowed lead to the goblin numbers drastically reduced. Goblins were never the "give and be done with it" kind of creature like the pixies and elves. No, they were the "giveth must receiveth" type of sorts.

After risking their own exposure in the humanoid world, they had to take something back in return, something of equal value or close to —a human or more specifically, a male. Someone to work the mazes for eternity.

2: THE HEIST

After a year had passed, the happy family lived together in peace and quiet. Not a single goblin scoured their home for crumbs or pets, in fear the half-breed would still remember them.

The goblins of today are now bound to their cog's cave and underworld realms but, on occasion, they must hunt, which requires time to be frozen, a magic even the goblins dread using. They're not the most agile of creatures or known for giving back. But the goblins had come to their wit's end, labour is limited and a boost in progress is required.

Throughout the towns and cities spread across England, the heist was about to take place.

With more children interested in finding out if the news is true and if goblins indeed existed, or even dragons. I haven't met a dragon yet, and I would be excited to do so. Wishes and dreams were pinged to me at a rate far higher than before. Thus, meaning more magic was being used to protect our under realms, and the goblins overworked. It seemed only fair to them that they take up their rightful trade of human male workers.

The England headquarters communicated with the control rooms throughout the country to organise teams to sneak into the houses at night and grab the men. There were specifics, but with their vision impaired in the humanoid world— even with vision enhancing, leather goggles—and a poor sense of smell, it remained harder than they expected.

In groups of three, the goblins, three-and-a-half feet tall, marched their way to the bolted goblin doors, protected by the pure magic, which opened with a series of twists and turns that clanked like steel. They were on the hunt for men, and only men, of a small build, and they must sleep on the left side of the bed, for superstitious reasons. It took three goblins to secure the males.

The goblins froze time, aiming to safely collect as many males as possible without any issues, but their magic was not as powerful in the human world, and had failed before. Precautions had to be made using a magic cloth to gag their mouths and a vial of paralysis to make them limp for the move back to the Goblin Kingdom

Even the law of time affects the goblins. Being powerful beings, yes, they could manipulate time, but they must give back whatever they borrowed. This means working all hours of the night collecting crumbs, fixing loose screws, and cleaning up after themselves. Someone had to keep up the work of the lost Peedie Folk, allergies or not. It was certainly not going to be the mythical creatures. I do not think they would get away unspotted. You never know when a half-breed will be about, so understandably, the goblins had to be cautious, in case they could sense or even see the goblin trails, for the extent of their powers were unknown.

The night had come, and the goblins clanked and scuttled their way through the red-bricked archway, walking straight through the walls as if it did not exist. Oblivious to their own racket, which they had no control over, goblins are not the most agile of beings. Hunched back, scaly, and green, packed with a satchel and tools, presumably prepared for any possible threat or event.

They slobbered through the kitchen floor, leaving trails of clay and sweat. Stairs were something goblins had yet to master, for they had no need. The three goblins walked in a line next to each other. It worked quite well until they came to the corner landing, where, as they turned to go up the next flight of stairs, they squished between the walls. Personal space was unknown to them. More clanking of their tools, which strung over their shoulders, rang through the house.

"Shh," said Loosebuttons.

"Ooh, you shh," said Coldbrew.

"No, all of you shh! We're nearly there. Get the vial ready," said Ironhelm, the leader of Section Olrom, HQ 5.

As their shadows crept to the parents' bedroom door, Ironhelm 'spat and shined' his shovel to poke it under the door to see who was on the left. It was Greg.

In they went like bandits on a mission. One leapt up onto Greg's chest and gagged him whilst the other injected him with the paralysis potion. The other blew magic dust at Wanda to prevent her from waking. They had tied his legs and arms together, and blindfolded him so he wouldn't be able to find his way out of the maze should he escape. They dragged his body without any care, opened the front door, as humans can't walk through walls, and entered back into their maze lair. That was the last time Greg was ever to see daylight again. To the goblins surprise, they had completed their mission.

****

As you could imagine, the Fox family were distraught—Father gone with no word or reason. Police could not find him, and they even concluded that perhaps he didn't love Wanda anymore and found somebody else, or simply couldn't stand being a father again and left. The twins daren't speak to Mother about it or express their feelings, in fear of making her withdraw to her study for days on end.

As the years went on, the twins were now eleven and grew somewhat distant, which was unfortunate, as they were now living in the countryside, two hours away from the city life in a faery tale-style cottage, with a garden bigger than any city home could offer. As I watched the children grow, Clara in particular, strange things began to occur.

With little entertainment and now home schooled, they only had each other.

Nora believed that something very suspicious happened to their father, but Jerry never liked to think about it.

After the event of the kidnapping, I kept a close

eye on the children and became fond of them—strange as they are, I've never quite understood humans, but they seem to be stuck in a very unfortunate situation and things keep getting worse. Suspicions were on the rise.

"How can she lie? She's only five and doesn't even talk," said Jerry.

It was as though Clara was conserving all her energy into using her telekinesis powers rather than talking. It was an unnecessary way of communicating for her. All she had to do was flutter her lashes and Jerry would come to her aid.

"She's manipulative," said Nora, "you should see the way she looks at you behind your back, with her snake-like eyes."

"Don't be so mean, she's our sister." Jerry observed Clara playing with their cat, her hands wrapped around its neck. Jerry smiled at her.

"But is she? Really? No, I didn't think so." Nora scowled at Jerry.

He frowned back and blurted, "She's more of a sister than you are!"

Nora seemed hurt, her eyelids turned red and

swelled. Although she never cried, you could tell she wanted to.

Jerry and Nora rarely spoke from that day on.

Blame seemed to be a constant battle in the family. With their father gone without any warning or understanding, their lives began to breakdown.

The creaks in the doorways got louder and the rustling during the night was closer. Even Clara became somewhat unusual, her uncontrollable desire to lunge her mouth around the cat's tail and constantly chase it with hunger in her eyes, became an obsession, more so than for most five-year-olds.

Clara was still unaware of her biological engineering, and had an unsettling essence about her. Nora did not enjoy being alone with her, but Jerry, on the other claw, enjoyed her company. It was his only company. She too was an explorer, and they would spend hours outside building dens and getting into mischief. Whereas Nora, now at the age of rebellion, spent her time moping and contemplating the meaning of life and trying to understand it all at once. Her hair remained the same, straight black with a morbid blunt fringe.

Nora, now with braces, her once wonky teeth were now on their way to being straight, which the faeries always reminded me was their doing.

Wanda now spends her time locked in her study writing away nonsense, leaving Nora forced to take on the role of mother—she cooked, she cleaned, she organized, she read books to Clara reluctantly. All Jerry cared about was himself and getting his next adrenaline spike out of the way. He was too busy to notice the strange goings-on.

Nora was a very meticulous being. She noticed and pondered virtually everything, and after the mysterious disappearance of her father, she was on guard. She knew something was not right, and it had to do with dearest Clara.

The country lifestyle offered peace and tranquillity, a perfect place for an 11-year-old girl to solve a mystery or two. With the constant screeching of cats, the strange blowing of winds, the creaky doors, and the shadows in the daytime, there was something more going on than the normal old, eerie house story. Nora knew Clara was not normal. Her silence was disturbing, yet her knowledge was profound—that of an adult— and could read and write perfectly. Clara was able to bring things to her that she needed without any effort. One minute a key to the back door would be on the kitchen ledge, far too high for her reach, but with a blink of an eye, the key would be in her hand. Nora noticed these strange goings-on for the past five years, but no one else would believe her. It was as though she could disappear without a trace if she wanted to.

Only Jerry understood Clara's silent language. His willingness to understand her made them closer. If she liked or disliked something, he could tell just by her eye movements.

As Clara would shift through the house at speed, her glasses would edge toward her upturned nose and rest there.

"Oh, Clara, you look ridiculous," said Nora as she poked her glasses back in place. Nora sniggered. Since the early reading age of two, Clara had the need to wear glasses. Without them she was almost blind, but it didn't stop her exploring.

3: GOBLINS' SECRETS

As winter settled in and cocooned the Fox household, they were bound for many days at a time inside. The house was old, ancient in fact. No one had lived there for 50 years, which was very noticeable, filled with cobwebs, an icy chill, rooms locked away, and wallpaper ripped at every seam.

Why was it empty for so long? I hear you ask. Well, it just so happens to be sitting exactly on top of the goblins' Section Olrom HQ 5, who have full control over who is allowed to reside there.

This was the perfect house for a young boy's

exploration, but the only thing that interested Jerry so far was a stethoscope, which from what I've gathered is an instrument doctors use to hear a heartbeat. He wore it constantly, like his prize necklace, his secret instrument to hear through walls. As he made his way through the entire house, knocking up and down on every wall, he listened to the odd sounds that came from them.

"Nora, I'm sure something is behind these walls. Some are hollow, some are hard like stone, but this one ..."

Jerry glared at Nora and said, "I can hear a dripping and muffled roars and clanking, all coming from in there." He knelt down with his ear to the wall, listening very carefully, trying to show Nora, but every time she went to listen, there was nothing there.

"Now who's the liar?" asked Nora.

"I promise, there's something under this house, I just know it."

Nora rolled her eyes and realised the house was too quiet.

"Where is Clara? I thought you were watching

her whilst I made the lunch?"

"No, you said you would watch her!"

Nora's mouth dropped, and Jerry leapt up, leaving the stethoscope behind him as they panicked around the house in search for little Clara. It was now the evening and still no sign of her.

Nora and Jerry had yet to tell their mother that they lost the little one, but the time had come. They both edged towards to the solid oak door with a large keyhole big enough to cover most angles with a clear visual.

Wanda, tapping away on her typewriter, still old-fashioned like that, was oblivious to anything that went on outside that door.

"Go on then, knock," said Nora, "You're the one that lost her."

Jerry scowled and stretched out his fist. Ratatat, he knocked in a cheerful manner, hoping it would reflect his mother's mood.

"What is it, Jerry?" She knew exactly who it was.

The door creaked open and a musty smell wafted through. Nora covered her nose and mouth whilst trying to be discrete.

"Um ... It's Clara, we can't find her," said Jerry. "Oh, don't be silly, she's probably hiding. Have you checked under her bed?"

"Yes," said Nora, "we did, and the entire house."

"And the garden," said Jerry.

"She will turn up," said Wanda.

"But ..." The twins didn't know what to do next.

"Now leave me in peace, thank you." Wanda pushed her glasses back up from her nose and began to tap away again. It was up to Nora and Jerry to find her.

As the day crept by, Nora's motherly instincts were far greater than her *own* mother's. There had to be somewhere that they hadn't searched yet where they would find Clara.

They scoured the entire house again. Nora took the top floor and Jerry the lower. With many rooms' locked and hollow sounding walls, he believed there had to be a secret passageway or secret rooms.

"Perhaps Clara's hiding in one of these, her tiny fingers could unlock the doors," said Jerry.

Using his stethoscope, he knocked on the dusty wallpaper and followed the seams until he felt a hole, a hard metal keyhole, similar to the one in his mother's room. With excitement, he ripped the wallpaper off, leaving a cloud of dust in the air. It was an old, solid oak door. He peeked through the hole, but there was nothing but blackness.

"Clara, where are you?" he said. "I know you're here somewhere."

Jerry knocked on the door to see if she would answer, but there was no response. He pushed with all his weight, as it flung open he fell face-first into the darkened room. There was a strange stink about the room. Jerry was not afraid of the dark, but his imagination always ran away with him, so his need to find a light switch was gaining on him.

He patted the walls around the room. Nothing but an old chain hung from the ceiling. He pulled it, and a dim light turned on just above a fireplace, revealing a room stacked high with books. There were a few old leather-bound books, which intrigued him. One titled *Goblin Secrets* and another called *Obey Your Boundaries*. Old trinkets, bells, and whistles were among dolls clothing left in a box next to a larger box, filled with all sorts of old Victorian style clothing and props. One object in particular caught his eye—a pair of goggles, leather-bonded with a strap. They were heavy, like no other pair of goggles he had held before. As he rummaged through the boxes, the stench became stronger. With a book under his arm and goggles in his hand, Jerry swiftly left, back to the corridor.

"Nora, have you found anything yet?" he shouted down over the railings.

"No, just dust and crumbs. This house really needs a cleaning!"

"You're so pedantic sometimes," he said.

Nora crossed her arms and huffed, "Well, it's getting late. I think we should get some rest and hope she turns up soon. We should tell Mum we've not found her yet. I don't think I could sleep if she didn't come home tonight."

"Aww, so you *do* care," said Jerry, mimicking a baby.

"Of course, she's our sister."

As they went to go see their mother, there was no response at the door. They found her asleep at her desk with a brown bottle of something by her side.

"Well," said Nora, "she's no use like that. I'll stay awake, you go to bed."

"Ok, wake me up if you hear anything."

Jerry traipsed back to his room and put on the pair of goggles. It took a minute for his eyes to adjust. As his eyes focused, he saw a complete new world. The goggles view was as though he were in a computer game, another world within his room. The walls stripped from wallpaper and filled with old books engraved with golden gears. His room revealed without a carpet or a bed.

"It looks so cold in here."

New doors appeared, and four child-sized throne-like chairs made for children staged the room.

Jerry plucked the goggles off his head and his room went back to normal.

"Wow that is by far the coolest gadget I've come across."

With his goggles resting on his forehead, Jerry flipped through the pages of *Goblin Secrets*, and the book landed effortlessly on page 11.

The first paragraph read:

It was always a competition. Any flickering lights in sight or in the corner of their eyes and they will be there in a flash, much like a cat.

In any occasion, it is undoubtedly safe to say that this is their weakness, an addiction if you like, a secret that goblins still believe to be kept today. If every goblin were to find the source of the flickering, all geysers would blow. The mining and engineering would stop. Magic would be gone.

Jerry's eyes drooped and the book slipped from his limp hand to the floor.

Nora, sat alone in her father's rocking chair, waiting anxiously, staring at the door, hoping her sister would walk through. As the hours ticked away, there was nothing but eerie creaks and scuttles throughout the house. With what has been going on in the news of late, Nora reminded herself she was never one for conspiracy theories, but the half-breeds intrigued her.

The wind moaned under the door like a ghoul. Nora tapped her fingers faster on the wooden armrests. She wasn't frightened easily, but a loud cat cry was the last straw. She sprung out of the chair, leaving a glow of dust in the light, and leapt into bed with Jerry.

"Did you hear that?" she said.

"No, I am sleeping! Did Clara come home?"

"No, she's still out there somewhere," replied Nora.

"It's OK, she will turn up, she's a tough cookie." Jerry squirmed and rolled over. Nora's nose scrunched up, it had been a few years since they had shared a bed. As Morning rose, the dreaded birds screeched at their window. It was as if something startled them at 7am every day, without fail. I suppose the goblins could be responsible.

Nora's colour drained as she turned a pale shade of yellow, she remembered their sister had gone missing.

"Right, let's go find her."

"Oh wait, look what I found last night," Jerry said as he grabbed the pair of goggles and put them on.

"Whoa, it's like I'm in a different land, you should see." Jerry wafted them towards Nora's face.

"No, I'm OK, they look terribly dirty," said Nora.

"Yes, but it's like magic. I can see doors that aren't there and flaky luminous trails ... all the way down the stairs."

"Oh, Jerry, your imagination is wonderful." Nora sighed and slipped on her shoes as she left for the stairs, dressed in her white nightgown.

"Breakfast?"

"Oh please, some oatmeal and jam?"

"Well, that's all we've got, so I guess so." Nora walked off into the kitchen and tied on her apron.

"The flaky trails have stopped. You really should look, and even the stairs have changed. Our home looks like a home for tiny people, with old desks and mini thrones ..." Jerry looked around for Nora, but she had gone.

"No way," he said, fixated on the fireplace. "I wonder what's behind that door."

Jerry had not moved from that spot for several minutes, the goggles seemed to have awed him. As Nora walked into the lounge, their dog appeared, barking and growling. Nora flung the bowls of oatmeal all over the carpet and into the pocket of her apron.

"Where did you come from?" she said, trying to calm the dog down.

"He ... he came through that door." Jerry pointed toward the fireplace.

"There's no door, just a fireplace."
He shook his head and passed her the goggles.

"Oh crikey!" said Nora, "There is a door. I think he wants us to go through it?"

"Ya think? Come on, let's go, pass me the goggles," said Jerry.

He stepped forward toward the door and prized it open. Nora stood in front of the fireplace, without the goggles she couldn't see the magic that unfolded before Jerry.

4: INTO THE COG'S MAZE

Jerry had disappeared. Nora panicked. "Jerry, where are you? Come back."

A hand appeared through the back of the fireplace, a ghost-like apparition of sorts. "Grab on," he said.

Nora dusted off her apron, looked behind her, and could not believe what she was about to do. In that very moment I received her first prayer. I am sure it was only a throwaway sort of prayer, but I will take it seriously, as I always do. Oh, and no, I will not share what she asked for, that is personal, just like a birthday wish.

Nora reached for the hand and scrunched up her face with anticipation, not knowing where she was going.

Jerry pulled her through the door and out the other side.

"Jerry, I can't see a thing, its pitch black."
He pulled off his goggles and said, "Put these on, you *need* to see this."

She slicked her black hair behind her ears and placed the goggles over her eyes. The goggles mechanically twisted and adjusted to her vision level.

"Are you serious?" Nora was not best pleased with the other side of the door. "You expect me to go through there? I'm still in my nightgown! I'm not cut out for this kind of stuff."

"If you want to find Clara, then this is our best bet." Nora sighed as she got on her hands and knees and followed Jerry through a tunnel filled with dust and rocks.

"Here, you'd better have these back." Nora patted his legs up ahead to pass him the goggles, wafting more dust in the air. The tunnel went on—

it was approximately an eight-minute crawl through rocks, dust and debris. An unsettling moaning sound echoed through the tunnel. A clanging and the sounds of metal clashed against each other, instilling an eerie atmosphere.

"What was that?" asked Nora, "See anything?"

"Well … Let's just say you'll be glad you're not wearing the goggles."

"Why? Tell me now!"

Jerry coughed, as every time he spoke he inhaled the dust.

"It looks as though there are pipes made from a golden metal travelling through the tunnel. Whatever that sound was, came from inside these pipes."

"What's so scary about that?"

"Well … The other thing is the trail of luminous flakes, like the stuff in the house before. I don't think we're alone down here."

"I'm going, *right* now." Nora tried to turn around in the tunnel, but there wasn't enough room.

"Typical! But you'll never make it back without

the goggles." said Jerry, "Keep up."

"Where are we going?" Nora asked.

"To find Clara, have you forgotten already?" Jerry stopped abruptly.

Nora crawled into him. "Ouch! What are you doing?"

"Shh ... I just saw someone ... or something," he replied.

"Maybe it was the dog?" she whispered.

"I don't think so, it had two legs, and it's left that scaly trail again." Jerry gulped, his breath growing shallow as the dust filled his lungs.

"Hold onto my ankles, okay? We can't lose each other down here. There's sure to be a turning soon."

They scrambled onwards, and to their relief saw a turning. The tunnel widened as a yellow light shone in the distance. Jerry contemplated the left path, which was not as luring.

"It's pitch black left, and there's a light up to the right. Which way do you think we should go?" asked Jerry.

"I'm not too keen on the dark, so let's head to

the light."

"That's what I thought." He cricked his neck and could breathe a little better now.

"Stay to the side of the tunnel, we don't want to be seen," said Jerry. They trudged onwards down the right pathway. To their relief it was a bit more spacious—the walls had widened, and the tunnel was broader. The soil was well trodden in, a path used frequently.

As they made their way creeping along the edge of the wall, the light that shone ahead was becoming clearer. Metal piping weaved out through the walls and bent into an ornamental light casing, to encapsulate a small bulb at the end, clearly the engineering work of the goblins.

"These are like the lights in our hallway. Odd ..." said Jerry.

"What do you suppose lives down here?" asked Nora.

"Take a guess ... You know the answer. You're just too naive to believe it even though *you're* the one that lives in those books."

"Don't be ridiculous. The news always lies, and

there is no way we have entered the goblin lair. I read to escape our boring lives, not to pretend the goblin lair is real!"

Jerry still lead the way, his fingers running along the wall to gain a sense of the goblin kingdom, which he believed they were now trespassing in.

"If the news was correct, and the myths and legends that we were taught in school had some truth to it," said Jerry, "Then this has *got* to be it. What other explanation is there?"

"A simple one," replied Nora. "Our house is on top of grimy tunnels that are proven to be all over London *anyway*, and I was stupid enough to follow you down here. There are no such things as goblins ..."

He sighed and gave up trying to convince her. Once she had made her mind up about anything, there would be no chance in winning the argument.

There was no sign of company since they made that right turn, but it had become clear that something lived within these tunnels. A skilled blacksmith had intricately woven pretend windows framed in metal. It was a window with a view, only visible when lit by a tiny light bulb representing the sun. Flowers and cats were bent into shape, almost like a cultural symbol, like the parietal art—cavemen drawings.

"How bizarre," said Nora.

"I'm guessing whatever lives down here doesn't get to see the sun much. I wonder where they get their electricity from," said Jerry.

"You do think of strange things, Jerry."

"No, I'll have you know it's a pretty logical question."

"Oh, look over there … a door."

Jerry leapt in front of Nora. "Where?"

A small round door made from metal and wood, held together by mud—a door only a child could fit through with ease—came into his line of sight.

"It's about my height." Jerry stood with his back against the door to measure himself against it.

"Yes, a children's door, I see." Nora was a whole foot taller than Jerry, something she always enjoyed pointing out. I never did understand why height was so important to children. After all, the faeries are tiny and are no less powerful than the dragons. Jerry reached his hand above his head to mark his height, when a loud horn sounded. It was an unearthly sound, best described as metal grinding against metal, echoing through the tunnel. The twins jumped away from the door and backed onto the opposite wall. As they leaned against it, the wall in front moved, like a merry go round. The right path now completely blocked off, and the door ahead had vanished. The tunnels were alive.

"What the heck was that?" asked Nora.

"It sounded mechanical. These goblins sure know how to create."

Nora tutted and said, "Seriously, which way now?"

The only path they could take was back where they just came from. Their pace quickened, and they knew that they had to keep moving just in case the walls changed again. Jerry, still leading the way, about ten steps ahead, tripped over something and landed face down in mud.

"You alright, Jerry? Get up."

Nora jogged towards him when she saw an emaciated cat lying on the ground.

"Ewe, you tripped over a cat! A dead cat!"

"So, the rumours are true." Jerry dusted himself off and wiped the mud from his mouth. The cat had been gnawed at, its hair mangled and bloodied. It was as though whatever was feasting upon this innocent creature was interrupted.

"We gotta keep going." Jerry grabbed Nora's hand and kept her close around the next corner. *I can't lose another sister*, he thought. There was just one path to take yet again, the curved wall seeming endless. The sound of clanging metal drew closer, and this time it was not in the pipes, but with them, in the tunnel. The twins edged back around the curved wall and Jerry thrust his palm across Nora's mouth. They could not risk being exposed.

The sound grew louder, a marching cadence pounded through the tunnel along with a mechanical tick and moan, which echoed through the tunnel. Jerry peered around the corner to see was ahead. Three goblins march with bowed, scaly legs, and a shovel in tow. They wore matching goggles and leather straps, which holstered their tools.

He shuffled Nora back down the tunnel. The moaning noise deafened them. As they crouched down and covered their ears, the wall shifted with a jolt and clunk.

Jerry reluctantly opened his eyes, in fear of the worst.

"We must have moved with the walls, we're in another room, take a look," said Jerry, relieved.

5: THE CONTROL ROOM

Jerry gawked in awe as he spun around the new room. A pleasant twist in fate had transported them to safety. Nora still cowered against the wall in a room filled with dusty leather-bound books, shelved to the ceiling.

"Nora, come on, take a look, you will love this." Nora peeled her hands away from her eyes. She gasped at the number of books.

"This is what my dreams are made of!" She ran her fingers across the spines of the books.

"None of these books make sense to me."

Jerry was more fascinated in the large well in

the middle of the room, which had golden pipes leading along the ground to a wall filled with gears. Wheels turning at a continuous pace, the well bubbled and steam rose to the ceiling.

"What is this ...?" asked Jerry, his eyes glistened with excitement.

Nora made her way through the books, with her head tilted, curious about the illiterate titles on the leather spines. This was the first time she smiled in a few days.

"Hmm, what did you say?" Nora backed towards Jerry and turned around to see what the fuss was. As she turned to him, the well exploded with a giant gush of hot water and magic—a bright golden light spewed from the well. The wheels on the wall sped up as though they were powering something. They had found the magical geysers, the source of the magic within the underworld, harnessed and utilised throughout the headquarters and nine realms.

They stood covered in golden dust. Nora stared at Jerry, waiting for an explanation, as this seemed to be his 'sort of thing'.

"Well … what do you suppose that was?" she asked, wiping her apron down.

He clung to his stethoscope like a doctor giving orders. "I couldn't possibly say, but I am certain this is a power station. See over there?" Jerry pointed to the table in the corner filled with electricals, radios, and buttons.

"I think this is where the goblins communicate with each other."

"Couldn't possibly say, hmm?" said Nora.

Jerry was in his element, all things technical and mysterious. He stared at the buttons and radio dials.

"This is ancient. I wonder if it works."

"Don't touch anything!" said Nora in a panic.

"Why not?"

"Goblins … That's why!" Nora planted her hands on her hips.

He frowned. "Oh, so you believe me now?"

Her cheeks flushed. Jerry's hand had already moved toward a dial sparkled with magic. Nora cringed with anticipation. A crackle and the sound of interference burst through the radio.

"What did you do?" asked Nora.

"Nothing!"

The interference turned into grunts and groans. The twins edged forward to listen in on the conversation.

"This is Commander Ironhelm of Section Olrom HQ5. We have been informed of intruders, yet again in HQ5. All goblins are required to stay inside your section of the maze. I repeat all goblins are to stay inside the maze. All other sections are locked down and there will be no access until the intruders are dealt with. You know the protocol. All missions to retrieve human DNA must abort immediately. Return to your HQ. Humans have breached, humans have breached! They are looking for a humanoid and will stop at nothing. Their shadows are that of giants and have magic powers of their own. This cannot be another war. No more goblins shall die today. Now go and disgust them."

The twins glared at each other in fear.

"Do you think they mean us?" Nora's voice

had changed to an unusual squeak.

"Most likely." He coughed to clear his throat.

"Disgust?" asked Nora.

Jerry shrugged his shoulders.

The radio crackled and muffled with the sound of a receiver.

"Tango that, sir. Goboid is contained and prepped." Between the crackles and fuzz, a cry of a child screeched in the background.

Nora and Jerry leapt back from the radio in shock.

"That better not have been Clara," she said.

"I bet you my shoe it is, we have to get out of here!" He searched for the nearest exit through the hazy room. Nora's gaze lingered at the bookshelf, which was barely visible anymore. She bit her lip in desperation of owning such a masterpiece.

The goblins of the magical realms and engineers of the cog maze are creatures that do not feel fear. Their only emotions felt are that of disgust and boredom. These feelings feed their desires to create and instil as much disgust into whoever happens to invade or jeopardise their existence.

With little feeling or emotion, they were bred to be slaves of the underground maze, to work and to protect. With their small frame and nimble fingers, a life bound to dig and perform services of a magical, mechanical engineer, was well suited.

As Jerry reached around the room trying to find the exit, his hands patted against a wall. The goggles, still on his head adjusted to his vision, allowing him to see through the fog. He had come quite accustomed to them. As the goggles focused, a map emerged on the wall, gears interlocking with each other that spread out across the entire London underground. As he looked closer, Jerry noticed the gears were the goblins' maze, with the Section Olrom, HQ5 pinpointed in the centre of the map.

"Nora, come take a look at this. We must be here." He pointed to a golden pot, which resembled the geyser in that very room, "Didn't they say we were in Section Olrom, HQ 5 ... This is us!"

Nora peered closer as the steam was fogging her vision.

"So, we're here … What's that house symbol?" asked Jerry, "It looks a lot like our home, don't you think?"

"It couldn't be?" replied Nora.

"They know we are here, that is *our* house, on their map!" Jerry gulped, and his palms began to sweat.

"It makes sense now."

Nora interrupted, "Oh my goodness … This map spreads out all over Europe. Look, there's France, Belgium, and Finland."

His bushy eyebrows rose high on his forehead.

"This is big, really big." He tried to his hide his nervous smile. He never did know the correct way to react, but then who does? He laughed when scared and cried when happy. Jerry shook his head and tried to focus.

"It's not just Europe." He pointed to a large group of cogs with thousands of HQ's marked. "If I'm correct, that is Northern America and the States … This is a worldwide problem." Jerry pulled out his phone, zoomed in with the camera, and took a picture of the map of London.

Rather clever, I thought.

With tunnels and access not only across the entire London underground but the whole world too.

"If Clara is down here, she will be in their most secret place, would you agree?" asked Jerry.

"Yes... But where would that be?"

Jerry pointed to a golden crown located on the map. It was four gears away from their current location.

"I can only guess that this is where their leader lives, or works. It's a start?"

"Ok then." Nora nodded and blinked a few times as she tried to concentrate through the steam.

"Right, where's the door?"

Jerry and Nora walked around the entire room, patting the walls, but the door had disappeared. The steam was clearing up and the room became visible again, but still no sign of the door.

"How can a door just vanish?" asked Jerry.

"I bet the walls moved again." Nora had a twinkle of excitement in her eye.

"If the goblins know we are here, and then they wouldn't want any walls moving," he said, "As it would be almost impossible to find us?"

The gears on the wall began to turn faster, and the well bubbled.

"I think we're about to witness another eruption," said Nora, as she backed away to the bookshelf and grabbed a book to hide behind.

Jerry remained on the other side of the room by the controls. As the bubbles rose higher and the cogs turned faster, he shouted, "Look out for an opening. When this erupts, I'm hoping the maze will shift gears and the next wall will have a door so we can get out of here!"

"Ok." Nora rolled her sleeves and kept her eyes wide open through the clearing steam.

"Ready... 3 ... 2 ... 1." The geyser erupted just on time, the gears clanked and moaned, and the wall shifted.

"Over there!" Nora pointed to a small circular door, about a meter away from Jerry.

"Yes!" he said.

Nora looked behind her to say goodbye to the

bookshelf, but it had gone. Her hand still gripped the book, and without a bookshelf to give it a home, she slotted it into her apron's front pocket. She peered over to Jerry and said, "Good team work."

Jerry raised his eyebrows in shock at her comment. As he gave the door a hard shoulder nudge he flung through it.

"What did you do that for?" asked Nora.

"I thought it would be stuck." Jerry's cheeks flushed as he hopped to his feet. "Here we go again. Now where is the crown room from here?" He zoomed in on the map on his phone.

"If the cogs keep turning, how will we ever find the room?" asked Nora.

"There are only so many teeth per cog, we just need to be patient. We find the room and wait for the door. In the meantime, we keep quiet and don't get caught."

Jerry smeared dirt across his face, like war paint and pointed his chin to the ground. She chuckled and wiped dirt across her face too. "Let's go," he said.

6: CHAINS AND CRYSTAL CAGES

The hours ticked by, and the risk of capture ever increased. As they carried on their search for Clara, little did they know that in the darkest depths of the cog maze, Clara was caged. Engineered for secrecy and in hopes of it being impenetrable, which over the years the goblins have realised is not the case. With wild animals and strange beings wandering through, their boundaries were not set as well as hoped.

As I scoured the maze for any messages or prayers, I heard none, not even from little Clara. Her scent is unique, and fortunately for her, was what gave her away. Her goboid aroma—musty vanilla pods mixed with fresh newspaper smell—led me to the room guarded by the plump goblin named Mortimer. The door to the room had a metal plaque shaped into a beaker, engraved with the letters: DNA TRACKING.

This was not something I had hoped to find. Mortimer stood like a solid oval rock. His jagged, large ears reached the top of the tunnel and his leather holsters crossed his bulging shoulders. His belly hung below his belt, filled with sharpened tools, decorated with cat bones and fur. The goggles strapped to his head too tight, forcing his eyes to swell out of their sockets. His face scarred with flaky scales hanging from his cheeks, unlike the other goblins.

As I kept my presence silent and discreet, I overlooked dear Clara's situation. I was shocked to find a five-year-old child locked and chained within the goblins' Lemurian crystal cage, in the corner of the room. This Lemurian crystal formed thousands of years ago, mined by the goblins for centuries. Its colour is clear, which absorbs the darkness and when in a dungeon-like room filled with black dirt, the cage itself mirrors with black dirt. Lemurian crystal is a powerful source for the goblins. Not only is it strong and durable, it holds a magical element of healing and balance.

The goblins use this to their benefit to maintain strength and balance. Some creatures say as they have yet to master love or hate, a neutral state of emotion and mind enables them to live longer, without pain or jealousy.

Perhaps this is why the goblins have taken over the entire underworld for so long.

Clara's frail, spindly looking arms, very deceiving, spread across the cage. It was a frightful sight. A tube ran from her arm, which fed blood into a bucket below, labelled, 'Goboid—Section Olrom, HQ5'. I had never seen this sort of behaviour before from the goblins, only the rumours that spread through our under realms.

I hoped they weren't true. Her glasses had a slight crack across the left ocular, but it didn't seem to bother her much. Her odd contentment

with her new surroundings was a sign of trouble. I watched Clara for any signs of prayers or hopes so I could pass them on to the source for granting, but she did no such thing. She grew agitated as her gaze focused on a pile of bones across the room, and she began to scratch and drool with a burning desire for them.

The metal door guarded by Mortimer knocked and rattled as the locking mechanism opened one bolt at a time. In walked the scientist, with a stethoscope matching Jerry's, which hung around his neck. He was not as sleek as the other goblins. He was a rounded fellow, but not as giant as Mortimer. His bowed legs waddled towards Clara. He grinned, baring his sharp, broken teeth. A trail of luminous scales scattered behind him.

"Ah, Clara, yes?" His voice was deep, slow with a slight crackle, yet somewhat friendly. Clara was silent. She bent her neck to the left with a sullen stare in his direction.

"I am Fenchwick, do you remember me?" he asked as he walked towards the pile of bones stacked to the ceiling.

He picked up a pointed bone and began to pick his teeth in front of Clara, fur and dirt flicked into the cage. Clara shook her hair to rid any debris.

"You, my friend, are a special sort," said Fenchwick. Clara licked her lips and drool began to leak from the side of her mouth as she watched him suck on the bone.

"I see it has begun. It shouldn't take too much longer now. You are an evolver. Five years old, am I correct?" His eyes rolled around in circles as though he was excited.

Clara nodded. She did not break eye contact with that bone at all. Her mental and physical energy seemed to be draining for her to evolve, destroying her human traits, one by one.

"Goboids of my creation come of age around 15 or 16, but you are nearly there. Your skin is accelerating at a rate I've never seen before, and your eyes, well ... you always had the goblin flicker, even at birth." Fenchwick sucked up the drool from his chin back into his mouth. "Waste not," he said.

Clara frowned. She looked confused. Her body

twitched and shimmered the more he spoke to her.

"Your brother and sisters... Do you remember them?"

Clara stopped twitching and examined the cage. It was as though she had completely forgotten why she was there. She let out a shrill scream, just the once, and then stared back at the bone which hung from Fenchwick's mouth.

"You must be careful, child. You don't want to rip out this tube, it's for your own good. Your blood is very special to us—blood red and thick streaks of blue, now that is a rare case," he said with an eerie smile.

"You are a prize piece, my most pure of creations. Female, yes, that is a problem, but your body will have no gender differences. You will be pure goblin, as you should have been at birth."

Clara's eyes changed to yellow. She was evolving too quickly.

"No one will find you here, I will keep you safe. You are my family too. Your brother and sister are on their way, but have gained the attention of the goblin commander and have very little chance of getting here alive. But I will help them, I just need to complete this blood drain and ... Well, never mind the rest."

Fenchwick waddled towards a pile of cat bones in the corner of the room and picked out a large femur bone. Next to the pile was another map, similar to the one in the control room, but a larger map of HQ5. Fenchwick adjusted his goggles and his vision zoomed in on his location. He pointed his long nails on the map and drew a route to the control room.

He reached into the cage, and Clara snatched the bone and instantly chewed on it like a Neanderthal.

"I will be back. Shh."

Fenchwick left the room and nodded to Mortimer, not daring to catch his eye. As the door closed, Fenchwick traced his long nails from top to bottom of the door. The intricate metal designs and bars moulded together as the door locked.

Mortimer, none the wiser, stood like a stone and guarded that room. No one was getting in or out.

7: LOST AND INTERRUPTED

The tunnels were silent, no clanking in the walls or moaning cogs. The silence was unsettling, and had not occurred since they entered the tunnel.

After years of Nora distancing herself and ignoring Clara, her feelings towards her were changing.

"We have to move faster, the goblins are too quiet. We must find Clara." Nora tied her hair up in a loose bun, preparing for action.

Jerry smirked, "Awe, you do love her."

Nora's eyes welled up and she slid her back

down the wall and hung her head in her knees.

"What's the matter?" Jerry looked left and right down the tunnel to check for any goblins. He placed his arm around her back. "It'll be OK, I promise we will find her."

Nora sniffled. "It's just ... I was always so mean to her, calling her names and thinking she was weird. What if she ran away because of me?"

"You can't think like that. She is a strong kid, she has had you to look up to. Do you remember when Fritz got stuck up the tree in our old house?"

"Yeah, that cat was stupid."

"Yeah, she was, but you saw Clara's face when she was stuck and couldn't get down and you climbed up the tree, no questions asked and brought her down. Clara's face was so happy, and she will always remember that, I swear it. She looks up to you."

Nora wiped her tears. She had forgotten about that day, blanked it out completely because she found her mother passed out on the kitchen floor. Nora was always the one left to tidy things up.

"Yes, I remember. Why didn't you climb the

tree?"

"That was the summer I broke my big toe on that metal bar sticking out of the ground. Really hurt!"

Nora chuckled to herself. "Oh yeah, the broken toe. That was an odd summer …"

Jerry ruffled-up his greasy hair and took a breath in.

"Are you OK?" asked Nora.

"Yeah, just my lungs aren't too keen on all this dust."

Nora looked along the tunnel and could not believe their luck, or lack of it. "Why are you being so nice to me?"

"Look at where we are," said Jerry, "I can't have you crying, someone might hear you."

She had hoped for a better reason and nudged her brother to the floor. She smiled and stood back up to take a peek down the tunnel in hope of a clue in which direction they should take. As she turned around to grab onto Jerry, he had disappeared. She knew the goblins would hear if she shouted for him.

She whispered, "Jerry, this isn't funny."

Nora jogged along the tunnel to find the doorway they just left, but it had also disappeared. A dusty air settled to the ground, the cogs had turned in silence.

She was alone. "What do I do now?" she said.

"Why weren't there any warnings this time?" Nora regularly talked to herself, must be a human thing.

"These goblins must be smarter than I thought."

She took a deep breath in and dusted off her apron, scattering oats to the ground behind her. "I wish I had that map." She closed her eyes, and once opened she walked with force, as though a dose of courage seeped through her body. Nora power-walked along the tunnel, there were still no sounds, and no sign of Jerry.

She knew that the crown room was only four cogs away, and hoped she was heading in the right direction. She kept close to the wall and constantly checked behind her. The sound of cranks and bubbles echoed towards her, leading to a door. Nora felt reluctant to approach it, but knew there was a possibility that Clara was inside. She pressed her ear onto the cold metal door and grasped the crystal doorknob. It was sharp and freezing to touch making her flinch.

"Goblin magic." She scowled and tried to listen into the room. There were rustling sounds and a high-pitched meow. She heard a loud thump and a ring of metal. Her fears were indeed true.

She stepped away from the door in shock and did not like the idea of being that close to a goblin. A curious marking on the door caught her attention, a metal plaque shaped into a cat, with an axe by its side. This was not the sort of room she wanted to enter.

Nora swiftly made her way down the tunnel. Windows, lit by a bulb, lead the way, detailed with a large pointed wand of Lemurian crystal and a bubbling geyser.

"I wonder if these are checkpoints. I'm sure the goblins must get lost too." She traced the metal design with her finger and smiled. It was a very skilled piece of metalwork. "My dad would like these." Nora sighed.

She hadn't thought about her dad for a long time because it would hurt too much. Her eyes were welling up, but she held back the tears, and carried on through the tunnel. A fork in the path appeared up ahead, and she remained slow and cautious with her back shuffling against the wall.

A scuffling of feet and a slight ringing of metal was getting closer. Nora stood still, not knowing where it came from. Feeling nervous, she shifted her view, checking all around her, repeatedly. She was not equipped to come face to face with such creatures. In that very heartbeat, everything froze within the tunnel.

It was Fenchwick. He cast a freezing spell on her from behind, he waddled up close to her, and sniffed at her hair. He gawked at her as he paced around and stood in front of her in disbelief at her size. He licked his lips and rubbed his hands together, leaving luminous flakes in front of her shoes.

"I'm sorry, my dear, but it's for your own good." Fenchwick reached into his pocket and delicately pulled out a syringe. He stood on his tiptoes but could not reach her neck. The freeze spell does not work for long, and is a magic with limitations. He waddled back down the tunnel and returned with a rock as large as his belly, almost doubled-over with the weight. He showed a somewhat sensitive side and rested the rock by Nora's feet.

"Ah, that's better. You won't feel a thing ... right, now."

Fenchwick stood at Nora's head height and poked the syringe into her neck. He whistled as a liquid went into her blood stream, then he pulled on the syringe and took a specimen of her blood. He placed her vial of blood into his belt, capping it with a cork.

"Job well done." Fenchwick checked along the tunnel for company. "Good," he said and gave a little chuckle with pride.

Nora's mouth began to unfreeze. As her bottom lip moved to try to speak, her left eye became alert. She wriggled her fingers and the goblin stood back. Her hair began to slide down her shoulder as everything softened. Fenchwick clapped his hands with excitement as she became more animated.

Her right eye finally began to wake up and then her top lip, allowing for slight movement.

"You horrible little goblin!" Nora tried to walk towards him, but her feet were still frozen. The fight or flight response was activated and adrenaline rushed to her feet to charge at the goblin, but her legs still froze in place.

"What do you want with me?" she asked, her cheeks flushed red with anger.

"It's not you I want, it's dear Clara, but she hasn't got much longer left. I want to help you, I do." Fenchwick stood expressionless.

"How is this helping me? Let us all go. Where are Jerry and Clara?"

"Jerry ... I'm afraid has probably already been caught, but Clara is doing just *goblinny*. She is brewing like a delectable potion. Those Peedie Folk had some good traits."

Nora's face began to show expression. Her eyebrows frowned and her teeth clenched, full of rage.

Fenchwick's goggles clicked and twisted as he nervously checked the tunnel for others. As he looked back to Nora, his goggles adjusted again.

"Where did you get those goggles? You better not have hurt Jerry."

"No, No, No," he stuttered. "These are not Jerry's, they are mine."

Nora rolled her shoulders as she began to loosen up. She hadn't quite mastered a plan, but her heart rate was still high, along with her repeated mantra, "Oh God, oh God, oh God." She never did finish that prayer, so I'm not entirely sure what she meant, but I watched and waited as her body came alive.

The goblin backed away a few steps, knowing the spell would wear off any minute.

"You better run, you puny thing!" Nora darted towards the goblin and tripped over the large rock by her feet. Her face smudged with dirt and her apron now brown. She got to her feet and scattered oats in the air all around her. Fenchwick squinted and sniffed the air. He hadn't smelt that aroma for years. He began to scratch his rather pointed nose, and twitch it from side to side—with the size of his nostrils, I can only imagine what would project out after a sneeze. His eyes began to itch, but he could not scratch them through his goggles—he kept trying, but couldn't seem to take them off. It was rather interesting to watch until his goggles popped off his head and his eyes bulged out, inflamed. His scaly fingers and toes began to swell twice the size. He let out an almighty sneeze, which spewed luminous green sludge across the path, and dotted along the hem of Nora's apron.

Nora froze yet again, this time intentionally. She stood staring at the goblin in worry and disgust.

"What's going on?" she asked somewhat sympathetically, trying to hide her amusement.

Fenchwick tried to speak, but his lips had flared up and there was no room to open his mouth. All he could do was stretch out his arm and barely point. He backed away, pointing towards the left fork in the path, and waddled away into the darkness.

8: TURNED

Somewhere within the parallel gears and the mechanical cogs maze, Jerry crouched, cornered in an archway. He wrapped his body, including his head, under his oversized knitted cardigan. Peeking through a gap as though waiting for a goblin to come by—or by the look on his face, a ghost—but there was nothing there. He adjusted his goggles and gripped onto his stethoscope.

Jerry twitched with every step and flinched at the flickering bulbs on the walls, his own shadows and dust. Something had spooked him. A sweeping sound accompanied by a pant made its way closer.

By this point, he thought he was imagining things and kept on walking until he felt a hard stone jab through his army boots. He stopped by a hole in the wall lit up by a bulb so he could take the boot off. This window embedded into the tunnel walls and chiselled with a shovel and pickaxe, a skull and crossbones—not a welcoming window this time.

Jerry leaned on the metal bars, which held the bulb in place, trying to gain his balance standing on one foot. As he pulled on the bar, a clank, and clicking of gear teeth echoed.

"Oh no!" He wasn't sure what he had done, but certain that the noise was not supposed to happen. He quickly shoved his foot back in the boot before he took the stone out. The walls on either side of him rotated with an awful sound, like a loud groan in the sky from World War I.

Jerry stood in the centre of the tunnel, not knowing which way to go, but had to choose fast before a crushing reality would take place. He looked at the window with the skull and crossbones and shook his head, not a friendly path. He darted through the crack in the wall to the right and just made it into another dark tunnel.

There in front of him stood a black ball of fluff. It was his dog, Gus.

"Hey boy, you found me!" Jerry gave him a big hug, which left him with dust and dirt all over his face. He spat the fur out and said, "You couldn't have come at a better time, where have you been?" The dog puffed his cheeks with excitement as his tail wagged profusely.

"It must have been you I heard panting and shuffling in the soil. You have to be quiet, boy, OK? At least it wasn't the goblins."

Jerry crept along the tunnel with Gus obediently by his side until he gained a scent on a doorway, where he sniffed the ground and scratched at the door.

"Gus! Stop that, come here." Jerry patted his trousers and walked towards the door. He tried to listen in for any signs of goblins.

"I think it's safe." He reached for the handle, cold as ice. As he twisted it, it screeched as though forgotten for years.

He pushed on the door. His eyes opened wide in shock and said, "It's open!" He shushed the dog and grabbed hold of his collar so he wouldn't run in straight away.

"Oh my, these are smart goblins."

Jerry meandered through wooden tables layered in metal beakers, needles, and vials of blood labelled with names. He scanned the vials curiously, until he stopped. The blood drained from his cheeks.

"Clara!"

Gus let out a whimper of sympathy.

Jerry's face went from pale to a bright raging red within seconds. He slipped the vial of blood into the side of his boot.

"Let's go, Gus, I've seen enough."

To the left of the door was a metal box anchored to the wall, filled with files with the word "Goboid" followed by their name and a personalised barcode. He flicked through the names as brisk as he could. To his relief, Clara was not among them. He closed the door behind him and noticed the plaque engraved with a beaker symbol and a needle. He checked on the map for any possible match of location.

"Yes! We're here, Gus." Jerry pointed to his phone as if Gus understood. It gave him comfort knowing he was not alone. "The crown room is only two gears away. I think that is where Clara will be."

Following the map along the tunnel, Jerry pinpointed all the doors and their places on the map for reference. They came to a fork in the tunnel—the left was a dead end.

"I bet that wall moves!" Jerry looked to the right and noticed Gus had already run ahead. He didn't want to whistle or call for him.

"I can't lose you again," Jerry huffed. The dog headed in the wrong direction, away from the Crown room, but he knew being with Gus would be safer than on his own.

He jogged along the tunnel and caught up with Gus, who had stopped behind a corner wall, and whimpered again. "What is it, boy?" The sound of heavy breathing drew near.

Jerry began to pant, his heart rate peaked, and he coughed uncontrollably as he tried to catch his breath. Gus walked around the corner, his hackles raised, his lips pulled back and he snarled, baring his teeth as a goblin hunched before him. The goblin was larger than most, with a back as arched and craggy as the caves in the dragon kingdoms.

Gus held his ground whilst the goblin sniffed and drooled, staring deep into the dog's eyes. He twitched his head side to side as though he was trying to figure out what Gus was. The goblin dropped his pickaxe and spat out a cat bone, the hollow sound echoed through the tunnels. He knuckle-walked towards Gus, his pace quickened and his eyes widened with hunger.

Jerry desperately tried to catch his breath from around the corner. He peeked at the goblin.

I've seen that expression of fear before, it was the look of pending death. His breath became ratty and shallow as he rustled in his pockets to try to find a weapon or something he could use for protection. He noticed a light was flickering on the wall opposite him and looked down to see his stethoscope was reflecting off the light bulb. Jerry crawled around the corner and saw the goblin, now only five feet away. The boy froze and stared at his face. Behind the goggles and the dirt was the same glint in his eyes that his father had.

"It can't be." He was barely able to speak. The goblin snarled and sniffed him out. With Jerry's last breath and all of his energy, he managed to place the metal end of his stethoscope on the ground and reflect off the bulb, in hopes of distracting the goblin. The goblin saw the light. Jerry reached with his finger and flicked the metal end to make the light move. The goblin was instantly distracted until he saw the source. The goblin's body shivered with an emotion I had not witnessed before by these creatures.

The goblin was angry and darted for the boy. The dog barked and leapt on the goblin, but the goblin's strength was enormous, and he flung Gus to the floor and with a vexing look in his eyes, with his hands in a neck-throttling action, nothing could get in his way. Jerry, desperate for help and struggling for breath he suddenly stopped. I willed for him to look behind to see the rock. As he searched behind him, he saw it.

"Odd, I thought I heard someone say something." Jerry grabbed it and waited until the perfect moment. The goblin was there, face to face. He caught a glimpse of his dad's loving eyes. Jerry froze, mesmerised. He didn't understand how this could have happened. *He was taken by the goblins too?* He thought. The goblin grabbed him by the neck. Jerry looked at the rock in his hands and with all his might, cracked him over the head, knocking him out. It was as though it happened in slow motion.

Jerry was in a full asthma attack, his face was white and his body limp. Gus comforted him and licked his face until he calmed down and began to breathe more deeply again.

Jerry patted the dog as they gazed lovingly into each other's eyes.

"What are we going to do about him? He's my dad!"

The young boy rested his head in his hands, trying to understand how this happened.

"They must have taken him that night. All this time he was right here, under our home. What have they done to you?"

Gus tilted his head to the left and nudged the stethoscope on the ground.

"What do you want me to do with that?"

Gus walked to the goblin and nudged his hands.

"You're right, I can't leave him here. We have to tie him up and drag him somewhere to safety."

Jerry took a deep breath in and shook his head. He couldn't believe what he was about to do.

"I'm gonna need your help. He's still my dad under all that hunchback and dirt." He held Greg's hands together behind his back, which clicked with every movement. Jerry shuddered at the sound.

"OK, you're going to have to hold his hands together, Gus. Can you do that?"

The dog tilted his head to the side as though he was confused. Jerry wobbled his father's hands to show him what he needed to do. Gus opened his mouth and gripped Greg's wrists with his slobbery lips.

"Good boy!" Jerry wrapped his arms with the

stethoscope and stood back to observe the situation.

"Now what?" asked Jerry. He pulled out his phone and looked at the map. "Right, we came from here ...," He pointed at the door with the beaker and needle symbols on the map.

"We walked this way and then you ran this way ...," He traced their route along the map. "So we must be here. There is a room not far from here, the symbol on the door looks like a book. Better place than any, I suppose."

Jerry tried to pick up Greg from under his arms, his grip was sweaty and the smell of unwashed humans wafted to his nose.

"Ahem, I didn't think this one through ... We need to untie him ... I know, I know, but I can't carry him like this, we must be quick."

With all his might, Jerry dragged his dad through the dust and dirt as quietly and quickly as he could.

"The door should be just around this corner." Jerry was barely able to speak, and with sweat running down his nose, he wiggled the tip to stop it from dripping onto Greg's head. With all the dust, his nose began to itch. "Oh no ... A ... A ... Achoo." Gus and Jerry froze in anticipation, willing the drop not to wake him. Thoughts rushed through his head in that moment. Thoughts like, *did I hit him hard enough ... perhaps I killed him ... I hope Dad doesn't wake up yet ... Wow, you're heavy.* The guilt was creeping up on him for not trying harder to find his dad.

"Nora was correct. She knew something wasn't right." Gus whimpered and nudged Greg's black feet.

"Oh right, yes ... Let's get on with it." They came to the door with the books engraved on it. It was open and left ajar. Jerry dropped Greg to the ground with a thud and checked for any company. He noticed the room crammed with books after books and thankfully no goblins. He leaned Greg against the wooden table in the middle of the room and tied him up to the table leg with his stethoscope. Jerry took a step back and stared at his dad. "I'm sorry." They closed the door behind them, locking it automatically.

9: TRACKED

Nora shifted along the tunnel with her left leg dragging behind as it had still not recovered from the frozen spell. Nora was eager to make as much distance between herself and Fenchwick, and chose the left path down a dark and hollow way. It would be a frightful challenge for even those ghoulish of warriors, but Nora's will was strong. She took a few deep breaths and kept repeating these words as she walked along the tunnel in hope of light or a friendly door.

"It's OK, everything's fine, I'll be OK, It's just the dark, I can take on these goblins, they're only short." Her eyes had adjusted well to the darkness by now, and she could make out the arched ceiling and the cracks in the mud layers, which revealed the metalwork beneath.

A grinding sound was in the distance, like the sound of the cogs moving and the walls changing, but it was as though it came from a tunnel, far away. *Jerry, where are you?* She thought. The cog's maze power could never stop completely throughout the goblins' headquarters—that would be devastating. The goblins maze spreads across the entire underworld, with one HQ per country. At least one geyser within one goblins' headquarters must be harnessing the magic and powering the realms at all times.

As the creaking and grinding turned into a banging of metal, it was almost rhythmic. Was it a war cry or a warning? Nora did not want to stay around to find out. She backed away to find the next path to take. She began to feel her leg again, and gave it a good shake to prepare for her journey. She bolted with vengeance. With her book in her hand and a rock in the other, she was armed and ready to take on anything in her path.

As she darted around the bend, Nora and Jerry collided. They tumbled to the ground as her book and his goggles flew through the air.

"Oh, thank God it's you!" said Jerry. "I was getting a bit worried." He wiped a tear from his eyes.

"Were you crying?" asked Nora.

"Erm, no, you just ... got oat dust in my eye, that's all."

"Ok then. Well I'm glad to see you too. Any leads on Clara?"

"Not on Clara, no ..." He frowned and leaned in for a closer look at Nora.

"What's wrong?" She asked.

"What's that on your neck?" Nora squirmed, and flicked her neck as though a spider was there.

"Looks painful." Jerry swept strands of hair away from her face. "You're bleeding."

Nora hadn't realised what the goblin had done to her. She touched her neck, and then the pain kicked in. "Oww, that nasty goblin!"

Jerry looked at Gus with a worried expression

and then said, "Goblin! What did he look like?"

"Short and fat, goggles like yours, but he was very different when he left."

"What's that supposed to mean?"

"Well, I think I have the key to their weak spot … They're allergic to oats. You should have seen his face." Nora chuckled as she envisaged him blowing up twice the size all over again.

"I wouldn't laugh too soon. Look what we found." Jerry showed her the vial of blood with Clara's name on it.

Nora clenched her teeth grabbed the rock on the floor, and held it firmly.

"Wait," he said, "There's more."

"Well spit it out, we haven't got all day."

Jerry's eyes flickered with nerves. All he thought about on his way was how we would tell Nora that their dad was alive, but now that he came to it, he was a bumbling mess. He flicked his hands to shake off his nerves.

"It's … err … Dad."

Nora quickly butted in. "We don't have time for this. Dad's not important right now. You sure do pick your moments."

He began to rock back and forth, as his breath grew raspy and fast.

"Ok, Ok, calm down, it's alright, I'll listen." She patted his back and sat him down by the wall.

Nora looked him in the eye and knew it must be important, as he never talked about his dad.

"Right, go on then," said Nora.

Jerry tried to speak, but the words wouldn't come out as he had hoped. "D ... D ... Dad is alive."

"This should be interesting."

He shook his head.

"He's here, in the maze."

Nora shot to her feet in shock and paced in circle. "How? Why? Did he see you? Where is he now?"

Jerry gulped and acted sheepish. "We sorta tied him up, and left him in the library."

"You did what?"

"I know, but you see ... He's not Dad anymore." Jerrys eyes welled up again.

"Of course he is, are you sure it was him?"

"Yes, he looked me right in the eye as I knocked him out with a rock." Jerry flinched as he waited for Nora to thump him across the head like usual when he had done something stupid.

Nora sat down and held her head in her hands. "So you're telling me that our dad is here in this for goblin-saken maze, knocked out, tied up, and left alone in a library?"

He nodded whilst Gus covered his head with his paws in shame.

"Ok." She stood and made herself presentable.

"I am sure you had your reasons, but we must find him ... after Clara. He left us for years, so ..."

"Well, actually, I think he was taken that night by the goblins. You were right."

Nora held out her hand and said, "Phone, please." She knew there was no point wallowing in the past. She had to be strong and carry on finding Clara.

She zoomed in on the photo of the map and showed Jerry where she had been.

"So we know she's not here or here, we have to get to this tunnel." Nora pointed to the door with the skull and crossbones on it.

"Yes, we were close to there but there was a wall

in the way."

"Well then we must wait for them to move. Whatever it takes!" Nora rested her hands on her hips.

"Actually ... I have found a way to change the walls, follow me."

She smiled and felt as though they were getting closer to Clara, which meant closer to home. "Come on, Gus, keep up."

They strode with a clear mission, yet their enemy spread among them like rats in the underground. A high-pitched ringing and a sharp buzz penetrated Nora's head. She fell to the ground and tried to block her ears. She moaned and winced, finally the ringing eased.

"What is it?" asked Jerry.

She rubbed her ears on her shoulders as though they were itchy. "A loud ringing ... I can hear a buzzing and some sort of interference."

Nora held both hands out in front her to stop anyone from making a sound. She stood still, staring at the ground.

"*What is it?*" asked Jerry.

She shushed him again. After a long minute of standing in silence within the goblin maze and creatures descending on them with a warrant for their arrest, Nora looked at Jerry with amazement.

"That blithering goblin!" Nora stuck her finger in her ear and shook her head to the side. "I can hear him, Fenchwick. He's telling me where to go."

"Yes, I understand," said Fenchwick, *"In the human world, this is classed as an invasion of "Human Rights", but I'm afraid it is for your own good. Now listen carefully. I am in the control room you found earlier, and am all ears and eyes. You must not hesitate. I will lead you to Clara and navigate you away from any oncoming goblins. OK?"*

Nora hesitated. "Err, OK."

"Right, you must move now."

Nora grabbed Jerry's' hand and yanked his arm as she ran.

"Whoa, where are we going?" asked Jerry.

"Shh, Fenchwick is leading us to Clara."

"What do you mean? How can you trust him? He could be leading us right to them."

"He is our only hope, and he has Clara. Now be quiet, I need to listen." A fork in the path forced Nora to stop.

"Now where? Come on then, Mr. All Eyes and Ears."

"*Yes, yes,*" said Fenchwick. *"It's just that you seem to be surrounded. I'm trying to find you a safe exit."*

Nora rolled her eyes and looked around the tunnel for a sign. She usually uses her head in these sorts of situations, but she felt a strange sensation in her belly, as I refer to as intuition. She decided to go straight.

"This way. I just know it," said Nora.

"What do you mean you *just* know? Which way did he tell you to go?"

"Err ... This way," she replied.

They tiptoed along the tunnel, the path pitch-black, and without windows, there was no light to lead the way.

Fenchwick interrupted. *"Where are you going? I've lost you on the video screens."*

"We went straight ahead," Nora replied.

"Oh … well done. There is a door coming up to your left. You're going to have to hide in there for a few minutes, the goblins are close and they are hunting for you."

Nora patted down the walls looking for the doors. "Jerry, how are your goggles right now, can you see anything?"

"Yes, I can see just fine, thanks. Where are we going?"

"Look for an opening, and be quick about it."

Jerry jogged ahead and came to a door. He pressed his ear against the dusty threshold for any sounds of life inside. To his relief, the room was empty with few candles lit and the floor layered with cat bones. He covered his nose with his sleeve.

"Nora, I've found a door, but it stinks!"

"Get in, quick." Nora shuffled through the door.

"Well done," Slobbered Fenchwick, *"Now I will tell you when you can leave. I think I left some tail or paw in there somewhere. I get hungry, you see, during my experiments. You're welcome to have a*

nibble."

Nora snarled and coughed to clear her disgust.

"It's okay, we will save it for you."

Jerry sat on the ground and tried to catch his breath.

"So what are we doing in here?"

"Never you mind. Just trust me, please." Nora took a deep breath.

"*You have four goblins coming past the door, so you must stay quiet. They won't be long,*" said Fenchwick in a jolly sort of way. "*They seem to be loaded with armour and tools with a long scroll of paper. Stand as far back from the door as you can,*" whispered Fenchwick.

Nora shuffled back to the wall opposite the door and grabbed Jerry's hand, he was oblivious to what was outside that door.

"*They seem to have stopped outside your door and are sniffing at the air. Just hold on there, okay?*"

Nora glanced at Jerry and said, "I'm sure everything's fine."

10: The Hunted

A foul smell of goblin wafted toward the room as a scaly flake sifted under the door toward the twins. Jerry's goggles zoomed in on the door and he saw the shadows of goblin feet. He looked at Nora with fear.

"What the heck is that? Do you know?"

Nora put her finger to her lips and squeezed his hand tight. He grabbed hold of Gus' collar and stroked him to help ease his nerves.

The high-pitched ringing pinged through Nora's head yet again.

"*OK,*" said Fenchwick, "*They look like they are*

on the move. It turns out that the cat-bone odour is more potent than I expected. I should've thrown them out after the first season."

Nora rested her head on the wall with a sigh of relief. "We can go now, Jerry."

"It seems their warrant for your arrest is rather warranted with the number of laws you have both broken over the past ten years," said Fenchwick. *"You need to be extra careful. The moment you get caught I can no longer help you, and that means Clara too."*

Fenchwick was a well-spoken goblin compared to the others, educated you could say. As the Goblin Kingdom is the magical core, laws are important and distinguished in the very beginning for themselves and for the humans who may one day wish to find and delve into the nine realms. As it was Jerry's wish to venture into the unknown, which was one law broken right there. Interfering with the will of a half-breed to find their birthplace is also a law broken, no matter the reason.

"With only a few humans that have ever stepped foot in the maze," said Fenchwick, *"It is*

safe to say no human had ever figured it out. Whenever magic reaches its peak or a human is close by, the wheels and gears turn. It's like a security system, protecting all the secret rooms and living quarters and magic chambers."

"That must be the geyser-type thing we found in the control room?" asked Nora.

"Yes, that's correct. Our maze is an endless exploration, which only a goblin could solve. It is truly beautifully engineered, and only suitable for the likes of us goblins to swing a pickaxe and shovel deeper holes throughout the lands. I am here to help. It is my fault you are here. You want something I have and you hold something I want."

Nora was silent. She didn't want to worry Jerry. "Now do you believe we can trust him?" she said.

"I suppose so," replied Jerry. "But what's in it for him, why is he helping us?"

"Perhaps he's just kind. Perhaps he wants to make up for his past mistakes?"

"Hmm ... Sounds fishy to me." A crackling of interference irritated Nora's ear.

"*Maybe I should make myself clear,*" said Fenchwick, as he coughed and cleared his throat.

Nora stood with her back against the wall and waited.

"Go on then," said Nora as she reached out her hand so Jerry would stop.

"We're listening." Jerry tried to listen in on their conversation by pressing his ear onto Nora's, but there was no sound.

"*I have to say I have always been rather jealous of you humans. The freedom you have and the magic you possess is far greater than our own.*"

Nora frowned with confusion. *How can such a creature surrounded by all this magic envy that?* She thought.

"*I have yearned to be human since my mother died,*" said Fenchwick, "*Her stories of your life and adventures were more exciting than any other stories. I remember after she cleaned the Elm House of HQ8, she was glowing with a different sort of magic—love. She felt the joy and seasons of your world. It was her favourite house,*" *you see. She was the one Peedie Folk who happened to fall in love with a strange goblin engineer and, ta-da ... here I am. I don't belong here and have used science to fulfil my desire. But then you turn up, and I know you can help me become human."*

A snort and cackle transferred over the earpiece. It is common knowledge to the creatures of the Nine that Fenchwick had always wanted to be more human than goblin. I could only imagine his excitement for that dream to become reality. Nora, with her mouth agape, then explained to Jerry, "You'll never believe what he wants!"

Jerry shrugged his shoulders. "I bet I would, this place is bonkers."

"He wants to be human."

"How?" Jerry remembered the vials of blood and the room filled with experiments and folders filled with names.

"The blood, talk about mad scientist!"

"Yes, he was wearing a strange sort of jacket with a belt stocked with herbs and lavender, and vials of ... blood. Well, we have no choice, we have to find Clara, and he's our only way out of here."

Fenchwick interrupted, *"You need to run. Now. Go."*

Nora looked behind her and heard clanking of metal and snorts. "Jerry, run!"

They sprinted to the nearest corner, a fork in the tunnel. There was no exit, no doors or a place to hide.

"This maze is useless for hide and seek," said Jerry as he tried to make light of the situation.

"Not the time, we're being hunted."

Nora backed away further down the tunnel. *Please be a door somewhere,* she pleaded on the inside.

If only she knew I was watching, but if that knowledge were to seep out I would get into trouble. The clanking was closer. Jerry battled with Gus' collar to try to keep him from attacking the goblins.

"Down boy, they will probably eat you too," said Jerry. His pupils dilated and his palms turned clammy.

"We need to get out of here," he said. Gus was

too strong and darted along the tunnel towards the goblins.

"Gus!" The sound reverberated through the tunnel. Jerry covered his mouth in shock.

"We have to run, leave him." Nora sprinted around the corner, desperate to find a door, and didn't stop until they found one.

Fenchwick guided them. *"To your left, you have to run, there is a door. I can see Gus, it's not looking great I'm afraid. You need to keep going, they're catching up."*

Nora tripped on a rock, face down in the dirt. "Grab on." Jerry helped her up and dusted her down. As he looked up a door appeared. "There's a door ... Get in," he said as he shoved Nora through the door. There was no exit. The room was dark and eerie. With a wall of cogs and clanking, it seemed to be another control room.

"Hide! Now!" said Fenchwick.

"There isn't anywhere to hide, they will find us." Nora panicked.

Jerry scrambled under the wooden table, visible from every angle in the room.

Nora climbed under the table, looked him in the eye, and said, "They are coming for us. Just be brave." She nodded at him and gave a little smile.

Jerry sucked in his cheeks to hide his fear. A high-pitched ring shot through Nora's ear, followed by silence. Fenchwick was no longer there. The door flung open, the musty stench of goblin reeked through the air.

A grumbled voice said, "Grab them."

Two goblins with turned-up noses and rusted rope dragged Nora and Jerry from under the table, tied them, and gagged their mouths.

Nora kicked and squirmed, she was a lot taller than they were.

"Master, we have a live wire, what should we do?" slobbered Loosebuttons.

"If you can't control the beast," said Ironhelm, "Then *you* will have to give back the time, understand?"

He grunted. "Yes, sir." Loosebuttons coughed and spat phlegm across Nora and Jerry's face. He pulled a vial of dust from his leather belt, which held his potbelly in place. The cork popped off the top and into Coldbrew's mouth, who choked and snorted at Loosebuttons with a thug look about him.

With the dust blown into their faces, the twins became limp and lifeless.

"Right," said Ironhelm, "Enough of your games, let's get them to the dungeons."

Nora and Jerry awoke tied back to back on the hard-mudded floor. Gagged and unable to speak, they tried to see where they were. Nora stomped her shackled feet on the ground in anger, the goblins laughed and snorted at her efforts. Jerry was silent, the quietest he had been all day. He stared at the door and nothing else.

"Hello, boy? Are you with us?" said Coldbrew as he prodded Jerry with his shovel. The goblins sneezed and scratched their faces, scales floated to the dirt like feathers.

"It's her, Master. Burn it," said Loosebuttons. Ironhelm stomped towards Nora with his ghastly hands covering his tusked jaws.

"You don't need this here, girl." He ripped off her apron and grabbed a torch, which lit the room, he hung the apron over the flames. His usual angry lines changed as though painted over, it was almost a smile. The book stored in her apron fell into the flames and instantly burst into dust without the goblins noticing. Nora squirmed. There was no clearer proof of evil than burning books, even unknowingly, in her eyes.

Jerry tried to speak but could only mutter "W ... W ... We ..."

The goblins heckled and Ironhelm thrusted forward, nose to nose and mimicked him, "Y ... Y ... You *what*?"

Nora grew angry and ripped off the gag with her teeth.

"We only want Clara. Let us go and we will never come back. We've done nothing wrong."

Ironhelm grunted and said, "You wander in here and think you can get away with it? You have upset the balance and stolen our magic. It's not our problem you couldn't keep a handle on your sister. She would have ended up here anyway."

"That's not true. Her home is with us!" said Nora.

The goblins were not one for making conversation. Ironhelm rubbed his jaws as they began to ache with every word.

"What do you want with her?" asked Nora.

"She will enhance our magic. It needs a boost and she'll do just fine. She's a rare breed. We did well with that one, except she's female." The goblins cackled and pointed at Nora with wild and hysterical eyes.

Jerry wiggled and tried to escape from the ropes. He recognized the knot from his book of sea scouts and was able to untie it.

A piercing siren rang through the tunnels—it was an alarm—a goblin was out of his designated area. Ironhelm pressed on his ear and stood to attention. It was the commander of HQ LDN radioing them to seize the goblin.

"Right you are, sir, we're on our way," said Ironhelm.

He looked at the twins, his eyes narrowed. "We will be back, there's no way out of here, humans."

The goblins wretched with disgust at the thought of humans and slammed the door shut.

11: DIVIDED

"**N**ow's our chance," said Nora. "Quick, untie yourself!"

Jerry wriggled out of the rope, and his hands were free.

"Nice one," said Nora, "Now me."

Finally free, she ripped off the gag around Jerry's mouth. He flinched. "Ouch!"

"There's no time for pain!" said Nora as she rolled up her sleeves and awaited directions from Fenchwick.

"What do you suppose that alarm was for?" asked Jerry.

"Take a guess?"

Jerry, in too much pain to answer, shrugged his shoulders.

"Well, I think Dad may have just saved our lives."

"Let's get out of here." Jerry scrambled towards the door. It creaked as they peeked through the gap. "It's clear."

"Do you know where you're going, Nora?"

"I'm still waiting for Fenchwick to come back on the earpiece."

"Forget him, come with me." Jerry scowled. He had decided to change plans.

"No, we need to go this way, to find Clara."

"She's in safe hands you say? Well then let's shut this maze down for good."

"What do you mean?" Nora didn't like the sound of that.

"Remember the first room we found? I believe that is the control room, and if I stop those cogs from moving, the entire maze will stop and the goblins won't survive."

"No, absolutely not, that is not a plan. Getting

Clara and then out of here *is* a plan!"

Jerry butted in, oblivious to what she had said. "According to the map, the control room should be just around the corner. As long as we can find the window lever, we can get in and out in no time."

Jerry had been planning this for a while now. It was as though anything Nora said seemed irrelevant to him, compared to what he wanted to do.

"I don't like this," said Nora.

There was still no sign of Fenchwick. Jerry ran through the tunnel, adamant on his plan.

"Wait up, you don't know what's around that corner." Nora ran after him. As he pulled the window bar, the wall turned and moaned. He slipped inside. "Quick, run. I can't hold this wall."

She darted to the wall desperate not to leave him alone again. She squeezed through the dusty gap, barely making it through, leaving not even a book's width of edge-way.

Jerry rubbed his hands together with a menacing grin as he stared at the perfect mechanical cogs on the wall.

"Don't you think this is too good a chance to pass up, Nora?"

Nora looked at him as if he was completely mad.

Jerry leaned forward, staring at the cogs as they twisted and turned in perfect synchronicity.

"It truly is perfection," he said as his face became emotionless, his entire demeanour changed.

"What's happening with you? You love all this sort of stuff, you can't ruin it now."

Jerry didn't say a word. He bent down to the ground with his eyes fixed on the wall as he picked up a cat bone. He ran his fingers along the edges, it was about seven inches long—a rather *large* cat if you ask me.

"This'll do nicely."

"Jerry, you can't! Listen to me for once, will you? Are you really going to risk Clara's life?"

"Listen to you? Listen to you? I've done nothing but listen to you my whole life. It's my time now, and neither you nor Dad can stop me. Now move out the way." Jerry pressed his fist firmly into Nora's chest to keep her at arm's length as he flung the bone precisely into the cogs. A moan and grinding sound, like the engines on a ship, or the gods bowling. It was not like any other sound they had heard down there. The cogs slowly came to a stop as the bone splintered and held them in place.

"That oughta do it," said Jerry.

"It won't last," Nora snarled.

He tutted, "Ever the optimist, aren't we ..."

Nora did not understand what was going on with her brother. She had never seen him like this before. It was as though the tunnels had darkened his mind.

"What now, then?" asked Nora.

The lights went out, and they were in complete darkness.

"You didn't think that one through, *did you*?" said Nora.

"It's, err ... OK ... I have the goggles, remember!"

"Always thinking of yourself," said Nora.

"Their power must be running low," said Jerry, "It must be HQ. They're onto us, but they don't know we have better sight than they do!"

The sound of the cogs grinding on the bone was

getting louder, the pressure from the geyser bubbled.

"I need to put another bone in," he said.

"But it's dark, you could knock out the other one."

"I can see, it's okay. You might as well leave and let me get on with it."

"Fine!" Nora reached her arms out in front of her as she fumbled her way to the cold doorknob. There were still lights on down the tunnel, so she didn't hesitate to leave until a slobbering and heavy breath drew close.

She slammed the door shut and blocked it with her dainty body. "Jerry ... There's something out there!"

"Yes, I thought you knew everything with your magic goblin in your ear."

"So, this is what this is all about?"

"No!"

"We don't have time for this, he's coming now. I can hear him at the door," said Nora.

A grumbling, phlegm-infested goblin pressed his bulbous belly to the door.

Jerry pulled Nora's arms and guided her toward the table in the far corner. He whispered, "Duck under the table with me, stay here."

The door flung open. The heavy-chested rattling and flat-footed stomps filled the room as the goblin rooted to find the twins. He grumbled words and sounds that even the goblins couldn't understand. The goblin bumped into the table and knocked all the radios and files to the floor. Nora let out a small shriek. Jerry instantly put his hand over her mouth. The goblin growled and ground his teeth, the sound worse than nails on a chalkboard.

Within seconds, the goblin was on the floor, lying still. Jerry prodded it with his boot.

"I think it's dead," he said. Flakes settled to the ground as his goggles zoomed in. The rattling breath was no more.

"But that means ..."

A voice came out of the dark. "Ah, it works," said Fenchwick. He had injected the goblin in the neck and paralysed him with a new elixir he had created that same day.

"That should last a tunnel inching," he said. An expression used by the goblins, to estimate an amount of time. Yet, as time was not something goblins were accustomed to—distance, on the other claw, was more to their understanding. After all, confined to small underground spaces, I could imagine it would come in useful.

Nora sighed with relief and said, "It's Fenchwick!"

They scrambled out from the table in the dark and then instantly thumped to the floor. Fenchwick stepped over the twins, toward the cogs on the wall, and pulled out the bone. The metal chugging sound resumed with an eruption of steam. The cogs could finally breathe.

"That's better," he said. He grabbed a hold of the goblin on the floor and backed away through the door.

"It's for your own good, kids," said Fenchwick.

The door slammed behind him.

The room filled with chugging and steam, the cogs power flowing smoothly again.

After an hour passed out on the cold floor, Nora

awoke in a dazed state.

"What just happened?" asked Nora. The lights were back on and the room was clear of goblins.

"Jerry, wake up. We need to get out of here before we get caught." Nora nudged Jerry. As furious as she was with him, she still wanted him alive and by her side. She shook his shoulders vigorously.

"Wake up, now!"

Jerry rolled onto his back, confused as to where he was, and sat up instantly and bumped his head on the table.

"Ouch!" Jerry held his head in his hands. "That's gonna be a bump soon," he said as he rubbed his forehead.

"Um … You've got blood on your neck." He wiped his neck and instantly winced, panicked, and began to hyperventilate.

"Calm down, Fenchwick must have tracked you too. But it'll be ok." Nora stroked his back to ease his breathing as she did when they were younger. "Let's find Clara."

"Are you kidding me? Fenchwick is not our

friend," Jerry said in a breathy tone. "He's a psycho. Who in their right mind would do this to us? Do you still believe he is trying to help?"

"Yes, yes, I do, so let's go." Nora stomped towards the door and began to twist the handle. A loud crunch and a deep roar echoed through the tunnel.

"Please tell me that's not what I think it is." She turned around slowly in hope that it was the walls moving. The cogs stopped, left wedged yet again with another cat bone.

"I've said we need to cut the power. It's our only chance of getting Clara back," said Jerry.

"No, no, it's not. Please, shutting off the power could kill Clara! She is half goblin whether we like it or not."

Jerry's nostrils flared and his face turned pale, like all the hope in the world had drained from his body.

The sound of clanking metal and a marching rhythm drew near.

"Do you hear that?" asked Nora.

"I'm not deaf, let's go, now!" replied Jerry.

With the tunnel barely lit Nora peeked to the left and then right. The sound of marching had dissipated. To her relief they were heading away from the room.

Jerry took out his phone and checked their location.

"OK, we have to go left and then follow the tunnel about fifty yards, and HQ should be the next door, as long as the walls haven't changed."

As they took three steps away from the door, Fenchwick had caught up with him.

"Ah, you children are slippery ones. Come with me, I'll explain on the way."

"Ha, I don't think so. You've injected me, how can we trust you?" Jerry winced and pressed his hand on his neck.

"It was for your own good, you must see that. You are not wanted here. The goblins are coming for you." Fenchwick scrambled through his belt of goodies, pulled out another vial, and attached it to his syringe.

"I'm sorry, but I'm going to have to do it again, for your cooperation." With a quick jab, he injected each twin in the neck. They slumped to the floor in an instant.

"Lovely," said Fenchwick. He attached a rope across their waists and dragged their bodies through the tunnel, leaving a dusty trail.

12: THE GOBLIN SHIMMER

Mortimer, the giant, still guarded the arched doorway that held Clara captive. Fenchwick stood with his neck bent back as he locked eyes with him. A grumble and grind seeped from Mortimer's mouth. He snarled and thrust his head forward, toward the twins knocked out on the ground and tied with rope.

"Oh, you mean these two 'orrible urchins? They're my prisoners." Fenchwick drooled and acted more hideously than usual.

Mortimer let out a gurgle as though he trying to laugh.

With a push of the bulb's metal casing, the bars on the door elegantly twisted and unlocked. With a screech, the door opened.

Fenchwick dragged the twins to the far corner of the room, then waddled back to the door and smirked at Mortimer through the dusty air and closed the door.

Fenchwick hustled across the room, and said, "They are sure to wake up soon." Clara's eyes opened wide, her breath became quick and shallow with agitation, and she realised who was lying on the ground opposite her. With her arms tied to the cage and tubes flowing from them feeding blood into a bucket, her movement was limited, yet she made no sound.

"I know, I know, I seem like the bad guy, but you'll see, little Clara, everything's about to change."

The room was dark and cold, the crystal cages infused with dust and disgust.

Nora's feet twitched, and the chains rattled around her ankles.

"Ah, it's about time," said Fenchwick. He

grabbed a vial of something from his belt, gently dabbed the liquid on his finger, and softly pressed it on Nora's mouth. Within seconds, she woke up. She awoke with ease as though she had slept for days, completely oblivious of her surroundings. She wiped her mouth as she noticed the drips.

"What's this?" she asked.

"Just a herbal elixir to make you less ... what do you call it ... human ... no ... emotional."

"I don't understand. Where am I?"

Nora wiped the sleepy dust from her eyes and peered around, finally noticing the chains and Jerry still asleep on the ground, the blood oozed from his neck. Her tone changed as her reality kicked in.

"What have you done? Unchain us now!"

"Well, that didn't last long. Must add some more lavender next time," said Fenchwick. "You must listen to me. I am trying to help you, but the other goblins are getting suspicious and time is not on our side. I've used too much already. You both need to get into this cage. Can you help me lift Jerry in?"

"Why? Just wake him up."

"He does not seem as kind or cooperative as you, so my thinking is that he needs to be asleep until we get him in the cage."

Nora tried to shake him awake but there was no sign of movement.

"You see, you are much safer as my prisoners then my allies. You need to get into the cage by yourself or I can put you back to sleep."

Nora huffed and grabbed Jerry under his arms. "On the count of three."

Fenchwick nodded and bent down to grip his legs.

"One ... two ... three," said Nora. They shuffled toward the cage, hanging from the tunnelled roof on a measly rope. "Are you sure this is safe?"

"Oh yes, I built it myself, 100% Lemurian crystal and hemp weaved by the finest of harvester goblins. I suppose you haven't heard of them either?"

Fenchwick climbed into the cage, which hung a meter off the ground. The cage rocked from side to side.

"This is fun." Fenchwick smiled an emotion that was not of goblins.

"Well, you stay in there then," said Nora.

Fenchwick pulled Jerry inside and hopped back to the floor. "I don't think that would go down very well, do you? In you get then." Fenchwick held his belt firmly, giving it a shake as a warning of his powerful tools.

"Okay, okay." Nora climbed into the cage. Unable to sit down, she balanced her feet on the bars and knelt down. Jerry was still asleep.

A rattling from a cage nearby caught Nora's attention.

"What was that? Is there someone else in here?"

"Oh Nora, so naive."

"What do you mean?" She pulled the goggles from Jerry's head and placed them over her eyes as they adjusted to the room's light. A cage appeared about five feet away. "Clara!" A tear fell down her cheek as she realised Clara was no longer human.

"What have you done to her?" Nora gripped the bars and tried to reach Clara. "It'll be okay, Clara.

I'm going to get us out of here."

"My dear, this was not my doing. She wandered into the only place on earth that would accelerate and integrate her goblin side. You see, she cannot go back now. Once half-breeds come of age and wander into our lair, they will start 'The Change' into a masculine form, to enable more workers back into the maze. I got one thing right during the engineering process. You would label her a freak of nature, which is rather ironic."

Nora dragged her palms down her face and whispered, "What have I done."

"I promise I am here to help you. There is one way she can become her human form again, but without this one piece, her shimmer will fade."

"What do you mean?"

"See this cage here? One piece of the Lemurian wand can stabilise a goblin shimmer for as long as needed. However, it must stay with her, by her skin forever. For one second without it will cause her to take on an irreversible goblin shine."

"Oh, I see ... Well, can I take some?"

"You're rushing, stop rushing. That is one

human trait I am not too keen on having. I want to be human, not this miserable excuse for a goblin life. I've waited a long time for this."

Nora peered toward Jerry and tried to shake him awake, but nothing.

"Oh, why won't he wake up?" she moaned.

"He will soon, but there is something you need to know."

"What's that?"

"I have taken samples of your blood, as you know that is my job." Fenchwick chuckled to himself. "I ran some tests and it shows you and Jerry share the same DNA. I have a question for you, please answer truthfully."

Nora kept quiet.

"Are you a boy or a girl?"

"What an odd question. I'm a girl, can't you tell?"

"Well you see, we have completely wiped out females from the goblin realm, but half-breeds are still lurking places. We have run many tests over centuries, but with your blood being so similar with each other's. I'm afraid it's rather useless. We can't risk testing you and Jerry in case we mess it up and get more females."

"I don't know what you mean," said Nora, as she began to tap her fingers to her thumb as to silence her relief.

"Can you change your gender?"

Nora let out a laugh. "No, of course not. I couldn't think of anything worse, except for being locked in a cage."

Fenchwick was curious. He had never had the chance to test twin DNA. He knew they were precious and something magical would come from them but he promised their release.

"How are you going to help us get out of here?" asked Nora.

"Unfortunately, the knowledge of your DNA has spread to HQ and they are adamant in your removal to the Intrepidus Gorge. But I want to keep you alive, Clara too."

"And Jerry?"

"Yes, yes I suppose."

"I have your word?"

"Goblins' words are far and few, but in this case

I can offer you my word. Or better yet, the truth."

Leaning forward, Nora held onto the bars with her nose poking through.

"The goblins are on their way and they will want answers. You need to pretend you're asleep when they get here, it's your only way of staying alive."

"Ok, I can do that. And then you'll let us out?"

"You will need to sacrifice something so I can use it to give to the goblins in return for your escape, or they will kill me."

Nora gulped and was not keen on the idea of sacrifice. "What sort of sacrifice?" she stuttered.

Fenchwick waddled away toward a green drape, which covered the other half of the room. He pulled it back and revealed a body lying on the ground.

"Who is that?" Nora asked.

"Don't you recognise him?"

"No."

"Well that's a shame ... This is your father."

"No, that's a goblin!"

"Yes, this is the power of the goblin maze— spend long enough here and you will soon turn into one."

"So you didn't turn him?"

"Oh no, my dear, he did that to himself. The magic here is powerful. We can simply sit back and watch it destroy you." Fenchwick smirked.

The sound of the metal bars unlocking echoed through the room, and Mortimer's voice grumbled.

"They're here," said Fenchwick, "Quick, lie down and don't move."

Nora wiped her eyes and laid next to Jerry, the bars below made for a very uncomfortable bed.

The door opened forcefully and slammed against the wall. Three goblins walked in with slobber and pus oozing from their ears, eyes and nostrils as though trying to intimidate them.

"Dogs disgust me, I don't know why they exist," said Ironhelm, the leader of Olrom Section HQ5

"Ah, hello ... dog, sir?" asked Fenchwick.

"That mangy beast just ran off," said Coldbrew, "We had him, but he attacked us."

Nora sniggered at the thought.

"What was that?" asked Ironhelm, as he focused on the cage.

"The children, sir. I have caught them and am currently running tests now." Fenchwick adjusted his belt and rattled his vials to create a distraction.

Jerry began to wake up, the chains rattled. He sat up and gripped the bars, his eyes dark with deep circles around them and bloodshot, his face pale, quite the opposite of Nora.

Fenchwick injected his neck as quickly as he could before he could say or do anything.

"You bar ..." Jerry dropped back down to the metal bars, flopping next to Nora.

"They're still alive?" Ironhelm bared his tusk like teeth, gargled phlegm, and spat at Fenchwick's feet.

"They belong in the Intrepidus Gorge. Their magic is not wanted here. You know this Fenchwick! Their DNA needs to be sterilised. Get rid of them, *you hear!*"

Fenchwick stepped away and gargled phlegm as a gesture of some sort of understanding. He dare not spit back at him, as that would certainly lead to his death.

"Few more tests, but not long to go now, Sir."

"What are you doing with that one?" He pointed to Clara.

"She's getting stronger every minute. It won't be long until we can use her in the mines."

Coldbrew and Loosebuttons had a fit of hysteria, unexplainable sounds spewed from their mouths, as if given a new chew toy.

"Enough you pair of Tunnelwarts!" roared Ironhelm, holding a razor-edged sword to their necks.

"And him? That's the one that escaped the human?" he asked, pointing to Greg.

"All under control, Sir. Nothing to worry about here." Fenchwick stared at the ground.

"It's all disgusting, get rid of them ... Today. Our magic is wasted on them," said Ironhelm. He thrust his sword back into his belt but missed and stabbed his leg. It was as though he didn't even notice.

"Yes ... sir." Fenchwick tried not to laugh and made no eye contact.

As the goblins left, Coldbrew gave Greg a kick and banged on the cages with his metal staff. The door bolted behind them.

Nora sat up and chuckled. "I can't believe they're afraid of Gus."

"Who's Gus?"

"My dog, he's a lot smarter than they are. He's probably on his way to the control room right now to start the cogs again. He's a sucker for bones too. You would probably get along." Nora pursed her lips and put on a brave face.

"I've noticed Jerry is not himself lately. The maze is not a good place for humans. He's becoming unstable and I will get you out as soon as I can." Fenchwick used the elixir to wake up Jerry, and stepped away from the cage. "This isn't going to be pretty," said Fenchwick.

Nora crouched into the corner and waited for his reaction. He leapt up, his leg slipped through the bars, and he said, "Where the heck am I now?"

13: FAMILY REUNION

A buzzing sound drilled through Jerry's ear, that feeling you get before you yawn. His breath quickened with worry as he realised his new surroundings.

"Jerry, breathe ... It's okay, you're safe here."

He glared at Nora and said, "We are locked up in a cage. I don't know what your idea of safe is, but this shouldn't be it."

Jerry gripped the bars in front and tried to open the lock. Sweat and dirt lined his oval face.

"It's crystal lock," Fenchwick snorted, "You won't be able to open it."

"You're in the Goblin Realm now. Our job is to harness the magic and spread it throughout the realms. No one can get you out except for me. So please, calm down and listen."

Jerry reluctantly stepped back to the corner and tried to relax. "Give me those," he said as he grabbed the goggles from Nora's face.

"Oh look," said Jerry in a sarcastic tone, "It's a family reunion."

"What's the Intrepidus Gorge?" Nora asked bluntly.

Fenchwick grumbled. "You do ask a lot of questions ... It's a realm designed for the unwanted, the feared, and the leftovers. As you have already seen, our magic and creations, they will not allow you to go back to the Human Realm. The only place is with the creatures that will destroy you." Fenchwick sniffed at Jerry's feet, his pupils dilated with a thirst for science. The goblin shuffled off to his table filled with vials, he poured some sort of liquid into it and a puff of steam rose out of the top. He stirred the potion and walked back to the cages.

"So I have placed trackers in you both, on the outside of your necks." Nora and Jerry both reached for their necks to feel the tracker.

"Don't even think about taking it out, I need to know you will hold up your end of the deal. Clara will not last long back in your world. By the time she is fifteen she will need to make up her mind and decide where she wants to live, with you as a goblin or here with her own kind." Fenchwick's shoulders bounced gently up and down as if he was laughing on the inside. Jerry tried to open the cage with a kick of his boot, moving the cage only slightly.

Fenchwick glared at Jerry suspiciously. "I will let you leave right now. I've got your blood, but I need you to give me something more."

Nora looked over to her brother in hope of an answer, but received a shrug of his shoulders.

"What can we give him?"

"I dunno, books?" he replied.

"The other goblins can't read, no good," said Fenchwick.

"I know ... We can give you cats," said Jerry,

"Our town has a lot of stray cats, and no one would even know they were missing."

"That's a start." Fenchwick licked his lips.

"Are you serious, Jerry? We can't, that's horrendous."

Fenchwick butted in. "We would require enough cats for a few years, do you think you could do that?"

"Yes," replied Jerry without hesitation.

Nora couldn't believe what she was hearing.

"Wait a second ... So you need us to bring you cats for two years?" she asked.

"That's correct, and a body."

Nora's face turned white in shock. "What body?"

"I think you two can decide, as you know there are four in this room, and one has been here for a lot longer and is far stronger than the rest."

"But we haven't even had a chance to say hello to Dad yet." Nora felt anger inside. She knew something wasn't right when Greg left.

"What should we do?" asked Nora.

"I feel it's my fault he's turned into this creature ... I'm so sorry, Dad." Jerry closed his eyes and prayed the goblins would take him instead. Thankfully, these sorts of prayers are not in my power to grant.

"What about me instead?" He asked.

Fenchwick laughed. "With your blood? Have you not listened to what I've been saying, boy? It's a way out or death. You can't work here."

Jerry looked at Nora, then to Clara.

"We've lived without him for a few years," said Jerry, "Clara's got her whole life ahead of her. I vote we leave Dad here."

"Just like that? How can you?" A tear fell from her cheek.

"You needed an answer, that's mine … You know I'm right. We've already grieved for him, not a single word in years—obviously I know why, now. But … Look at him, that's not Dad anymore." Nora hung her hand in her knees and took a deep breath.

"You're right, you can have … Greg and the cats. Please let Clara go, Right now!"

Jerry huffed and tried to hold in his tears.

Fenchwick mixed another liquid into the vial, he

held onto it tightly and plugged it with a cork and tucked it away in his pocket. He then moved toward the cage, took the tubes from Clara's arm, and labelled the bucket: 'C-8.2/4-Almost'.

He rattled his belt and a sharp-pitched ding, rang.

"Ah, there it is." Fenchwick pulled out a small, sharp, clear crystal and began to saw at the bars on the cage. He sliced through the bars with only three thrusts.

"Here you go, she'll want this, its Lemurian crystal for her humanity. I suggest strapping it to her underarm or chest. One day without it, mind you, will do irreversible things. Be sure to remember."

He looked at the twins and said, "You have no idea how special you are," as he tapped on the cork top of his vial. Fenchwick slowly unlocked Clara's cage, as to deliberately add suspense.

Nora and Jerry clung on to the bars willing him to do as he said.

****

Free from chains and crystal cages. The twins

and Clara finally reunited, although certainly changed since leaving home.

Jerry was eager to leave the darkness and the dusty air. He grabbed Clara's hand, as he would before, yet this time her hand slipped through. Her muscles stripped to skin and bone and her see-through skin was veiny and cold. Her childlike nature had vanished. With one last glance towards Greg, Nora sniffed to hide her tears and Jerry saluted before they left the room.

Fenchwick grew agitated, his dream soon to become a reality.

"I'll be seeing you in two weeks."

The door creaked open as the wall shifted positions, the cogs were running, the lights flickered and buzzed.

"Hurry now children. Remember the path so we may meet again," said Fenchwick.

The wall slammed shut, dust filling the tunnel. In that moment, I was overwhelmed with relief, as I had been willing the poor children to safety for the last 24 hours; it was as though the twins sensed my sigh. They instantly stopped and glared at one another.

"What was that?" asked Jerry.

"You heard that too?" Nora flinched as she looked behind her to see where the sound came from.

Jerry nodded. "Odd. We should run."

He picked up Clara like a baby and sprinted his way along the tunnel filled with rotted cat bodies.

Nora covered her nose with her arm and carefully made her way through the bony minefield.

"I see a door," said Jerry.

"Let's hope it's the right one," His goggles adjusted and zoomed in on the door. An arched, elegant iron-crafted doorway was a welcoming sight, only twenty feet away.

A bark echoed along the tunnel, and the sniffing sounds drew closer.

Nora yelled, "Here boy, come on!" She tapped her knees, and out of the dust, Gus had found them.

"Good boy!" said Nora. "Show us the way home."

Gus galloped towards the doorway and began to dig into the earth below. Jerry rested Clara on the ground and tried to pull on the iron doorknob, but it would not move. Nora tugged and pulled on every bar hoping it was the key to unlocking it.

"How do we get home?" Jerry huffed and slumped to the floor.

"Don't give up now, we've come all this way—this must be it."

Clara, a delicate being, rolled onto her hands and knees. Her frail limbs dragged toward the door. As she pulled herself up with the bars, her body shimmered into the Clara we once knew. Her skin rushed with a shade of red, her eyes filled with the colour blue and life again.

Nora and Jerry stared with hope as she stood up straight. Her frame taller than before, she was strong. They watched in awe, mouths opened wide, waiting for her next move. Clara leaned in close to the door, peaking through the keyhole, shaped like a teardrop.

She knocked on the door twice and blew through the hole, and the door cracked and ice began to spread from the hole, across the entire door. It was as if Jack Frost had snuck into my story.

Beautiful shards of ice froze the door solid. Clara reached the handle and gracefully twisted it. The door opened, into their fireplace, back home.

As they clambered through the dark tunnel and out the other side, they closed their eyes with relief. Nora squeezed Clara and said, "Oh, it is so good to have you back."

"I can breathe fresh air," said Jerry, "Oh boy that feels good."

It was night time, the curtains were drawn, the light from Wanda's study shone from under the door. The house was silent.

"Let's go to bed, you need a good night's sleep, and we've got some cat hunting to do." Nora rolled her eyes. She could not believe the deal they had to make.

Nora tucked Clara safely into bed with the Lemurian crystal safely strapped under her armpit. She swept her hair from her face and kissed her goodnight.

"Come here, Jerry." Nora held him in her arms and said, "We never have to talk about this to Mother. I am here if you are sad or need to talk to someone. I am sorry for being ... you know ..." Jerry butted in, "My annoying sister? I wouldn't have it any other way."

He squeezed his sister and didn't say a word. As he peered over her shoulder, he saw a dark figure with a top hat on, leaning against the lamppost outside their house. Jerry walked towards the window and swept the nets away.

"Who do you suppose that is?" he asked.

"Oh, I don't know ... I'm off to bed. I've had enough for one day."

Jerry sighed as Nora crept away. His curiosity got the better of him, and he grabbed his goggles in hope of a better view. "Fenchwick!" As he took his goggles away, a man took the goblin's place. He was taller, human, and well dressed. "He did it!"

Fenchwick tilted his top hat and nodded at Jerry. He raised a vial as though he was making a toast to him. With a grin, he dissolved away, behind the lamppost.

When Jerry and Nora awoke the following morning, it took them a while to gather their thoughts and realise they had made it back home. Jerry sat up in his bed and looked around the room. *Did that just happen?* He rubbed his eyes, and yelled, "Clara!"

He ran into Nora's room, where Clara had spent the night.

"You're here. We actually did it."

Clara's face was full of colour, her cheeks pink from a rested sleep. As she sat up, there was no sign of the goblin flicker. Jerry picked her up and gave her a squeeze. Nora awoke and smiled, no words could make that moment better.

"How about that oatmeal now?" asked Nora.

Jerry and Clara nodded.

As they walked downstairs to their kitchen, someone was already cooking. Jerry froze and put his arm out to stop the girls. "What is it?" asked Nora.

"Last night I saw Fenchwick... What if he..."

Nora rolled her eyes and slithered toward the kitchen. "Mum! It's you."

"Of course it is." Wanda had not made them breakfast in over four years. Dressed with a lace apron, she served up three dishes of oatmeal, jam and brown sugar in the centre of the table.

Jerry and Clara peered into the kitchen, with relief they ran up to Wanda and gave her hug.

"How did you know Clara was back?" asked Jerry.

"What do you mean?" said Wanda. "You are my children. I had a terrible dream that I lost you all and just had to make sure you were all okay when I woke up. Now come on and sit down, breakfast is ready."

For the first time in over four years, breakfast time was enjoyable, and nothing beats having it made for you. Sometimes being a magical creature has its rewards more than just being a messenger.

Nora and Jerry locked eyes, and he gently shrugged his shoulders, they daren't say a word to spoil that moment.

"I picked some bluebells from our garden this morning and thought we could place them at Dad's spot after breakfast?"

Jerry sniffled. "That's a wonderful idea, Mum."

"Yes, I would like that very much," said Nora.

Clara nodded and slurped the last bit of the milky oatmeal.

"That's settled then."

Every other day, Nora and Jerry would scour the streets for any cat carcasses and bones left lying around and collect them in a large potato sack. Clara could know nothing about this, they were too afraid it would bring back unwanted memories.

Jerry took on the role of the deliverer, waiting for Fenchwick's shadow at the streetlight every other week.

The arrangement seemed to work, and Fenchwick was now half human, half goblin, at will.

There was not a night that went by where they didn't sleep with one eye open. Any shadows or sounds would wake them. Nevertheless, little Clara slept with ease.

Goboids are everywhere.

Turn the page for an important message ...

How to detect a Goboid in your home

1. They may possess skills of telekinesis.
2. May have an odd desire to sniff out, and/or, eat cats.
3. Flicker of the eye.
4. Usually the quiet ones
5. Possess the ability to freeze time.
6. Discretely manipulative.
7. Possess the ability to shape shift.
8. Shimmering bodies.
9. Receptive to emotions and highly sensitive.

If you find your humans have more than **six** of these traits, then you are more than likely to be in possession of a goboid. Proceed with caution.

Next in the *Nine Realms* Series

The healers have been telling tales of the past, and it is time to put things right. In a world of black and white, life becomes monotonous for Beth. Magic and myths are something only of stories, but in the small town of Pillar Rock, a magnetic and eerie presence keeps strangers away. But for James, it feels like home.

Four Pillars of the community have stood strong for decades, but now time is ticking for the Realms. Have the humans gone too far?

About the author

A.K. Baxter is the creator of the Nine Realms series and has published the For Goblins' Sake book, first in the fantasy, middle-grade series.

Whilst residing in the Okanagan, of beautiful British Columbia, Canada, the scenery provides a fantastic array of wonder and adventure—perfect for creating magical, fantasy tales.

Born and raised in Bournemouth, on the south coast of England, Annie has had the pleasurable influence of vast ocean views, new forest magic, and country folklore, which has influenced her style of writing today.

Annie enjoys working with children, teaching meditation and outdoor education, nature, and team building.

With her holistic approach to life and love of nature, Annie hopes to share her knowledge through her stories and provide coping tools for children through difficult times.

Mountwillowbooks@mail.com

Okanagan, BC, Canada

95067880R00105

Made in the USA
Columbia, SC
11 May 2018